Expand

雅思 IELTS 學術寫作關鍵字筆記

User's guide
使用說明

跟著學習步驟，循序漸進，雅思寫作能力定能跨步大躍進！

　　一本由「字彙」、「語塊」和「想法」組成的資料庫，協助學習者掌握單字的用法、累積對不同主題的想法、蒐集組織語意的架構，有效達成雅思寫作任務的單字學習書。

☝ 圖表寫作

❶ 讀完學習指南

　✓ 瞭解評分標準

　✓ 掌握學習方向

❷ 認識描述各類圖表的方式

　✓ 單字、語塊、搭配詞

　✓ 句型

❸ 完成練習題

　✓ 按圖表填入適當的字來描
　　述趨勢

　✓ 造句來熟悉單字使用

議題寫作

1 讀完學習指南
- ✓ 瞭解評分標準
- ✓ 掌握學習方向
- ✓ 釐清觀念

2 認識各類命題下不同主題的單字
- ✓ 內容性語塊
- ✓ 單字、語塊、搭配詞
- ✓ 常見錯誤

3 段落發展
- ✓ 內容性語塊
- ✓ 發展導論、正文和結論的架構

4 大綱
- ✓ 統整文章內容
- ✓ 累積有關不同議題的觀點

5 完成練習題
- ✓ 用填空練習提升對各類語塊的熟悉度
- ✓ 造句來對單字使用更加熟練

Preface 作者序

▋ 單字擴充導航

　　《Expand: 雅思學術寫作關鍵字筆記》是一本專為雅思學術組寫作測驗設計的單字學習書，當中不僅統整圖表與議論寫作的關鍵字，也引導讀者運用「語塊」和「段落發展」的觀念來重整學習單字的習慣及方法。

　　透過上述的學習途徑，本書帶領讀者達成以下目標：
　　一 . 掌握雅思圖表及議論寫作的高頻單字；
　　二 . 學習連結單字的意思及用法以強化記憶與理解；
　　三 . 釐清單字使用上的套路以逐步訓練仿效和獨立造句的能力；
　　四 . 培養出能用連結和辨識套路來學習單字的習慣，讓單字學習不再是硬背而是理解。

　　全書教授內容分為「圖表」和「議論」寫作。在圖表寫作中，讀者能學會描述有關折線圖中的趨勢、長條圖中的異同以及圓餅圖中的比例的一系列字彙和句型。議論寫作會透過範文中來說明回答各種命題的關鍵字，如：同意或不同意、優劣勢和問題與解決方法。除此之外，讀者不僅能認識討論不同主題會用到的字彙也可以累積多方的觀點來培養回應議題的靈敏度。

　　換句話說，「語塊」和「段落發展」是貫穿全書的核心也是擴充單字的基礎。語塊就是由字組成的小團體，它是承載一個字完整意思的單位，而母語使用者就是用這樣的單位來搭建每句話的訊息。例如：listen to 或 depend on 等。然而，非母語使用者對單字的學習大多停留在中英對照的層面，這導致多數人在寫作中經常發生誤用或是表達不完整等問題。本書在圖表寫作中就會用「語塊」來教導讀者描述圖表的單字和相關句型來讓他們能清楚並準確地呈現數據。

議論寫作的單字學習範疇更廣，考生不僅要會回應不同命題的單字，更要有足夠的字彙來發展各類主題的討論。這樣的狀況就需要再把語塊做更細緻的劃分，分成「內容性語塊」和「結構性語塊」來顧及這兩個學習面向。「內容性語塊」指的是在不同主題下經常使用的單字，像是討論玩具和孩童時，就常提到 attention span 或 hand-eye coordination 等。本書從每篇範文中篩選出與主題相關的單字作為學習的主軸，幫助讀者界定明確的範圍並熟悉字彙的用法。光是會使用單字不足以能寫出一篇文章，因此「結構性語塊」也不能被忽略。這類的語塊即是銜接、連貫、總結等用來組織語意用的架構，像是 I believe this opinion is… based on…reasons. 或 I am of the view that… 等用來表達和重申立場的架構。在範文的單字講解後，每回都會提供文章的導論、正文和結論等段落的發展架構，讓讀者的論述能條理分明。

本書就像是一個由「字彙」、「語塊」和「想法」組成的資料庫。在解釋單字時會說明單字的使用套路並提供一個沉浸式的學習環境讓讀者熟悉這些字彙在特定主題下的使用並列舉常見錯誤讓學生能審慎地使用單字。在統整與特定主題相關的字彙後，這個資料庫更會抓出範文中的「結構性語塊」，來讓學生將學到的內容（單字與想法）填入列舉出來的架構中，用模擬的方式來培養造句能力。在學習的過程中，讀者更能吸收不同議題的觀點來逐步開發批判性思考的能力。

因此，《Expand：雅思學術寫作關鍵字筆記》適合剛開始準備雅思對單字感到迷茫、已準備雅思一段時間想在寫作獲得突破，或是想瞭解能有效提升單字量及造句能力的讀者。這是一本能協助學習者掌握單字的用法、累積對不同主題的想法、蒐集組織語意的架構來有效達成雅思寫作任務的單字學習書。

Contents

目錄

Exercise①圖表寫作練習題

Exercise② 議論寫作練習題

・折線圖
・長條圖
・圓餅圖

I

圖表寫作

　　雅思官方的評分標準除了替應試者釐清各級分在任務達成（task achievement）、字句連貫與邏輯銜接（coherence and cohesion）、詞彙資源（lexical resource），以及文法準確性（grammatical range and accuracy）等四大指標的表現差距外，這套說明也能協助考生界定字彙學習的範圍並指引能締造佳績的準備方向。

　　四大指標中「任務達成」和「詞彙資源」的描述即為考生提供一份藍圖，以下讓我們用多數學校的入學門檻六級分（Band 6）來一探端倪。

　　這是「圖表寫作」的說明：

級分	任務達成	詞彙資源
6	■ 處理此項任務的要求（addresses the requirement of the task） ■ 呈現一個含有經適當挑選資訊的概述（presents an overview with information appropriately selected） ■ 呈現並凸顯特徵或要點，但其中的細節的相關性、適當性及準確性或許不佳（presents and adequately highlights key features/bullet points but details may be irrelevant, inappropriate or inaccurate）	■ 任務中使用的詞彙範圍夠廣（uses an adequate range of vocabulary for the task） ■ 嘗試使用較不通俗的字彙但其使用不正確（attempts to use less common vocabulary but with some inaccuracy） ■ 犯下拼字或字型變化的錯誤，但這些錯誤不影響文意（makes some errors in spelling and/or word formation, but they do not impede communication）

上述內容替圖表寫作的單字準備列出三大原則：

（一）要能彰顯各類圖表中的大趨勢及特徵；

（二）要能使用同義詞來避免重複的內容和用近義詞來更準確描述圖表變化；

（三）不能犯拼字或字型變化的錯誤以免阻礙文意的傳達。

若將這些原則與各類圖表特性並列，我們能更加明確地掌握學習的方向。例如：在練習折線圖時，務必要知道如何表達數字的上升、下降、持平與高低點；在演練圓餅圖時，就要注意描述佔據比例的方式；在準備長條圖時，就要學會呈現數值的差距等。除此之外，考生也要能在各式比較句型中正確使用這些單字或在串連文句時靈活運用詞類變化。他們要懂得按照架構轉變字型以符合文法，同時也得知道使用同義詞承接上下文或運用近義詞描繪不同程度的變化。換句話說，圖表寫作的單字準備，要聚焦於有關趨勢的字彙使用、字彙於不同句式中的型態變化，以及活用同義詞與近義詞。

折線圖

increase（上升）

本節的焦點為 increase 的使用，讀完後即能掌握這動詞的「語塊」和「搭配詞」以具體描述折線圖中數線的趨勢。

🖊 參考圖表

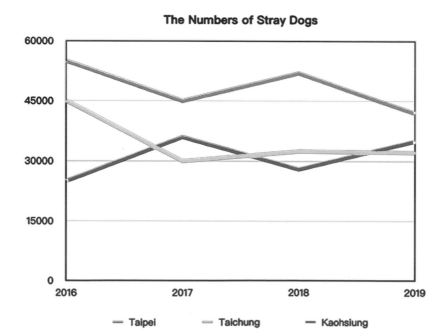

The Numbers of Stray Dogs

— Taipei — Taichung — Kaohsiung

常用語塊

看到圖表後，如果只能寫出 "The number of stray dogs in Taipei increased in 2017."，這樣的句子內容既不具體也無法展現語言能力。換句話説，如此的寫法無法獲得考官的青睞。我們要使用 increase 的「語塊」才能清楚地描述圖表中的數據變化，常用的語塊包含：

…increase to…	…increase by…	…increase from… to…
…to 增加後的數值	…by 增加後的差距	…from 增加的起點 to 增加的終點

使用範例

語塊	例句
…increase to… 在介系詞後寫入增加後的數值	In 2018, the number of stray dogs in Taipei increased to about 50000. 在 2018 年，台北流浪狗的數量增加到約 50000。
…increase by… 在介系詞後寫入增加後的差距	In 2018, the number of stray dogs in Taipei increased by 2000. 在 2018 年，台北流浪狗數量增加了 2000。
increase from…to… 在 from 後加上增加的起點 to 後加上終點	In 2016, the number of stray dogs in Taipei increased from 18000 to 34000. 在 2016 年，台北流浪狗數量從 18000 增加到 34000。

☝ 搭配詞

學會使用語塊來描述趨勢後，若能掌握「搭配詞」，寫出的句字將能變得更活靈活現。以下是常與 increase 搭配的副詞：

大幅增加的副詞	小幅增加的副詞
…increase considerably… …increase dramatically… …increase significantly… …increase dramatically…	…increase gradually… …increase slightly… …increase steadily…

☟ 使用範例

動詞＋副詞

■ **大幅增加：…increase dramatically/substantially…**

例 In 2016, the number of stray dogs in Kaohsiung <u>increased dramatically</u> from 18000 to 34000.

在 2016 年，高雄流浪狗的數量從 18000 大幅增加到 34000。

■ **小幅、逐漸增加：…increase slightly/gradually**

例 In 2017, the number of stray dogs in Taichung <u>increased slightly</u> from 30000 to 32000.

在 2017 年，台中流浪狗的數量從 30000 小幅增加到 32000。

rocket, soar（暴增、驟升）

本節將說明 rocket, soar 這兩個代表「大幅上升」的動詞，使用上要注意以下幾點：

釐清基本定義	✓ **rocket (v): to increase quickly and suddenly** 快速且突然地增加 ✓ **soar (v): to increase quickly to a high level** 快速地增加到某程度 根據以上的定義，**rocket** 的上升幅度比 **soar** 高。下圖第 3 條在 **2017-2018** 的變化就能用 **rocket** 來描述，而第 1 條線在 **2016-2017** 的變化就能用 **soar** 來描述。
避免語意重複	這兩個動詞本身就有大幅增加的意思。若再搭配先前教過的程度副詞，如 **dramatically, substantially**，就會重複語意。
活用語塊	語塊仍是會派上用場，回答以下問題來測試自己記得多少： ✓ …………… 增加後的數值 ✓ …………… 增加後的差距 ✓ …………… 增加的起點和終點

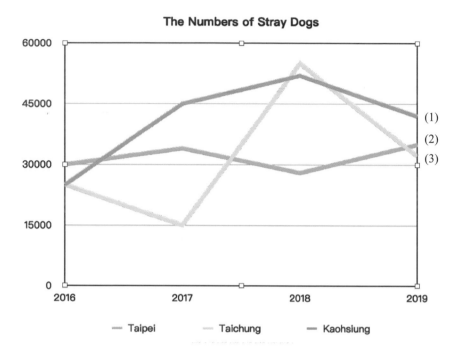

The Numbers of Stray Dogs

(1)
(2)
(3)

— Taipei   — Taichung   — Kaohsiung

🏆 使用範例

語塊	例句
…rocket by… 在介系詞後寫入增加的量	In 2018, the number of stray dogs in Taichung rocketed by 43000. 在 2018 年，台中的流浪狗數量暴增了 43000。
…rocket to… 在介系詞後寫入增加後的數值	In 2018, the number of stray dogs in Taichung rocketed to 58000. 在 2018 年，台中的流浪狗數量暴增到 58000。

…rocket from…to… 在兩個介系詞後依序寫入數值的起點與終點	In 2017, the number of stray dogs in Taichung rocketed from 15000 to 58000. 在 2018 年，台中的流浪狗數量從 15000 暴增到 58000。

語塊	例句
…soar by… 在介系詞後寫入增加的量	In 2017, the number of stray dogs in Taipei soared by 23000. 在 2017 年，台北流浪狗的數量大增了 23000。
…soar to… 在介系詞後寫入增加後的數值	In 2017, the number of stray dogs in Taipei soared to 45000. 在 2017 年，台北的流浪狗數量大增到 45000。
…soar from…to… 在兩個介系詞後依序寫入數值的起點與終點	In 2016, the number of stray dogs in Taipei soared from 22000 to 45000. 在 2016 年，台北的流浪狗數量從 22000 大增到 45000。

decrease (下降)

本節的焦點為 decrease 的使用，透過這動詞再次複習教過的「語塊」和「搭配詞」以更加熟悉趨勢的描述。

綜合複習		
語塊	程度副詞	
✍ .... 下降後的數值	大幅	小幅
✍ .... 下降後的差距	....	....
✍ .... 下降的起點和終點	....	....
	....	....
	....	....

✏️ 參考圖表

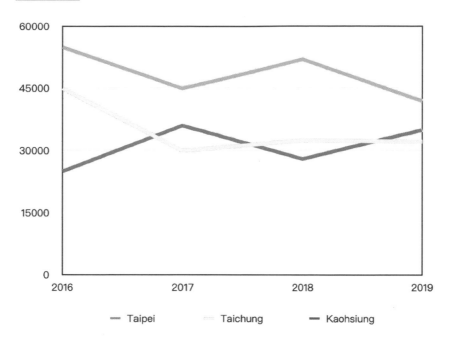

✌️ **語塊使用範例**

語塊	例句
...decrease to... 在介系詞後寫入減少後的數值	In 2018, the number of stray dogs in Kaohsiung <u>decreased to</u> about 28000. 在 2018 年，高雄流浪狗的數量減少到約 28000。
...decrease by... 在介系詞後寫入減少後的差距	In 2016, the number of stray dogs in Taipei <u>decreased</u> <u>by</u> 9000. 在 2016 年，台北流浪狗數量減少了 9000。

...decrease from...to... 在 from 後加上減少的起點 to 後加上終點	In 2016, the number of stray dogs in Taipei decreased from 54000 to 45000. 在 2016 年，台北流浪狗數量從 54000 減少到 45000。

🏆 搭配詞使用範例

動詞＋副詞

- **大幅減少 :...decrease considerably/significantly...**

  例 In 2016, the number of stray dogs in Taichung decreased from 45000 to 30000.

  在 2016 年，台中流浪狗的數量從 45000 大幅減少到 30000。

- **小幅、逐漸減少 :...decrease steadily**

  例 In 2019, the number of stray dogs in Taichung decreased steadily to 32000.

  在 2019 年，台中流浪狗的數量從小幅減少到 32000。

plummet, ebb

（暴跌、驟降）

本節將說明 plummet, ebb 這兩個代表「大幅下降」的動詞，使用上要注意以下幾點：

釐清基本定義	✗ plummet (v): to fall suddenly and quickly from a high level 突然且快速地從某高度跌下
	✗ ebb (v): to fall from a higher to a lower level 從高點跌到低點
	✗ 根據以上的定義，plummet 的下降幅度比 ebb 高。下一頁圖表第 3 條線在 2018-2019 的變化就能用 plummet 來描述，而第 3 條線在 2016-2017 的變化就能用 ebb 來描述。
避免語意重複	這兩個動詞本身就有大幅增加的意思。若再搭配先前教過的程度副詞，如 considerably, significantly，就會重複語意。
活用語塊	這些是目前介紹過的：
	✗ ...to 下降後的數值
	✗ ...by 下降後的差距
	✗ ...from...to... 下降的起點和終點

✎ 參考圖表

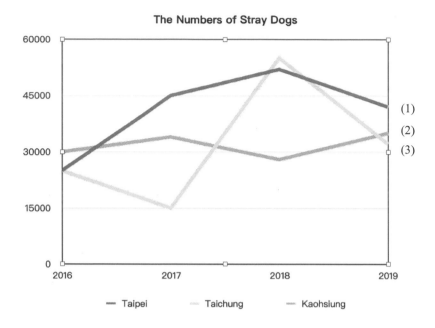

The Numbers of Stray Dogs

(1)
(2)
(3)

— Taipei   — Taichung   — Kaohsiung

☝ 語塊使用範例

語塊	例句
...plummet by... 在介系詞後寫入減少的量	In 2018, the number of stray dogs in Taichung plummeted by 22000. 在 2018 年，台中的流浪狗數量暴跌了 22000。
...plummet to... 在介系詞後寫入減少後的數值	In 2019, the number of stray dogs in Taichung plummeted to about 30000. 在 2019 年，台中的流浪狗數量暴跌到約 30000。
...plummet from...to... 在兩個介系詞後依序寫入數值的起點與終點	In 2018, the number of stray dogs in Taichung plummeted from 52000 to about 30000. 在 2018 年，台中的流浪狗數量從 52000 暴跌到 30000。

語塊	例句
...ebb by... 在介系詞後寫入減少的量	In 2016, the number of stray dogs in Taichung <u>ebbed</u> <u>by</u> 12000. 在 2016 年，台中流浪狗的數量驟降了 12000。
...ebb to... 在介系詞後寫入減少後的數值	In 2017, the number of stray dogs in Taichung <u>ebbed</u> <u>to</u> 15000. 在 2017 年，台中的流浪狗數量驟降到 15000。
...ebb from...to... 在兩個介系詞後依序寫入數值的起點與終點	In 2016, the number of stray dogs in Taichung <u>ebbed</u> <u>from</u> 27000 <u>to</u> 15000. 在 2016 年，台中的流浪狗數量從 27000 驟降到 15000。

reach a climax/a base, remain plane, fluctuate（高低點、持平、波動）

　　本節說明在折線圖中出現的其他趨勢，例句中都會用上學過的內容。我們要學兩個新的語塊，如下：

…at…	…between…and…
…at 固定數值	…between A 數值 and B 數值

🖊 參考圖表

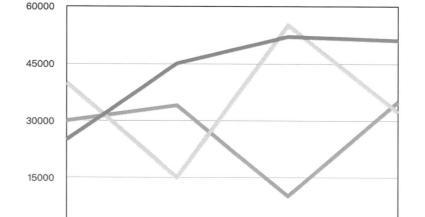

The Numbers of Stray Dogs

👆 最高點、最低點：使用範例

趨勢	例句
…reach an apex/a climax/a summit at 固定數值	In 2018, the number of stray dogs in Taichung reached an apex at about 55000. 在 2018 年，台中的流浪狗數量達到最高點約 55000。
…reach a floor/a base at 固定數值	In 2018, the number of stray dogs in Kaohsiung reached a base at approximately 10000. 在 2018 年，高雄流浪狗數量減達到最低點約 10000。

👆 持平：使用範例

趨勢	例句
…remain plane/keep steady/stay balanced at 固定數值	In 2018, the number of stray dogs in Taipei kept steady at approximately 50000. 在 2018 年，台北的流浪狗數量維持平穩約 50000。

👆 波動：使用範例

趨勢	例句
…fluctuate/waver between…and…	From 2017 to 2019, the number of stray dogs in Kaohsiung fluctuated between 32000 and 10000. 從 2017 到 2019 年，高雄流浪狗的數量在 32000 與 10000 間波動。

常用句型

　　本節講解描述折線圖時常用的句型來示範活用趨勢動詞及語塊的方式，這同時能協助讀者溫習句型組成的基本觀念，更能達到以下雅思寫作的評分標準：

■ 任務達成	能使用各類句型和字彙來具體描述圖表數據
■ 詞彙資源	能精準使用各類字彙來描述圖表趨勢
■ 文法正確性與廣度	能使用不同句型來展示對文法規則的熟悉和對句法的掌握

📝 **參考圖表**

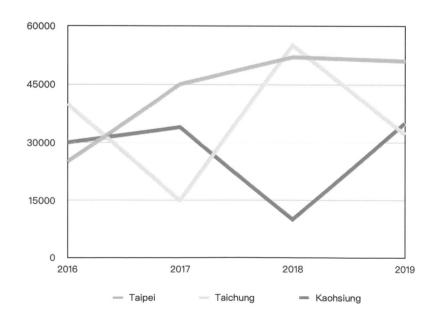

分詞構句

複習

- 使用時機：當連接詞前後的句子主詞「相同」時，可以使用分詞將句子簡化

- 簡化方式：保留「主要子句」的主詞、移除「從屬子句」主詞並將其動詞變成「現在分詞」（V-ing）、去除連接詞

- 範例

原句	分詞構句
The number of stray dogs in Kaohsiung increased from 30000 in 2016 **and** the number of stray dogs in Kaohsiung decreased substantially to 10000 in two years. - 對等連接詞 and 前後的主詞相同（底線） - 折線圖中時間點晚越晚的趨勢，重要性越高 - 因此主要子句在 and 之後，之前的為從屬子句	Increas**ing** from 30000 in 2016, the number of stray dogs in Kaohsiung decreased substantially to 10000 in two years. - 移除從屬子句的主詞並將其動詞換為動名詞 increasing - 去除對等連接詞 and - 保留主要子句的樣貌

» 句型（一）使用範例

Increasing/Decreasing from…, S + V.	
原句	分詞構句
The number of stray dogs in Taichung decreased from 40000 in 2016 and the number of stray dogs in Taichung rocketed to 56000 in 2018.	Decreasing from 40000 in 2016, the number of stray dogs in Taichung rocketed to 56000 in two years.

» 關係子句

- 使用時機：當兩個獨立的句子有「相同」的主詞時，可以用關係子句合併

- 合併方式：用「關係代名詞」取代其中一個句子的主詞把連接兩個句子

- 範例

原句	分詞構句
The year 2017 witnessed the most dramatic increase in the number of stray dogs in Taichung. The number of stray dogs in Taichung increased from 15000 to 56000. - 以上兩個獨立句子有「相同」的主詞 - 可以用關係代名詞合併	The year 2017 witnessed the most dramatic increase in the number of stray dogs in Taichung, which increased (=increasing) from 15000 to 56000. - 用關係代名詞 which 代替第二個句字的主詞來合併 - 第二個句子為第一個句子的「補充說明」，因此在關係代名詞前需要「加上逗號」 - 關係代名詞後加上一般動詞可以省略成「動名詞」（V-ing）

» 句型（二）使用範例

The year...witness/experience the most dramatic/substantial increase/decrease in 類別 , increasing/decreasing from...to...	
原句	分詞構句
The year 2017 witnessed the most substantial decrease in <u>the number of stray dogs in Kaohsiung.The number of stray dogs in Kaohsiung</u> decreased from 32000 to 10000.	The year 2017 witnessed the most substantial decrease in the number of stray dogs in Kaohsiung, **which decreased (=decreasing)** from 32000 to10000.

長條圖

same, identical, similar to

（描述相同處的形容詞）

　　本節說明長條圖中用來描述相同處的三個形容詞，學習內容包過釐清基本定義、熟悉語塊、以及使用代名詞來避免重複。

👆 基本定義

same (adj)	two or more things are <u>exactly</u> like each other
identical (adj)	<u>exactly</u> the same, or <u>very</u> similar
similar (adj)	<u>almost</u> the same

以上定義中的程度副詞（exactly, very, almost）能幫助我們排出這三個形容詞在相似度上的高低，如下：
same = identical > similar

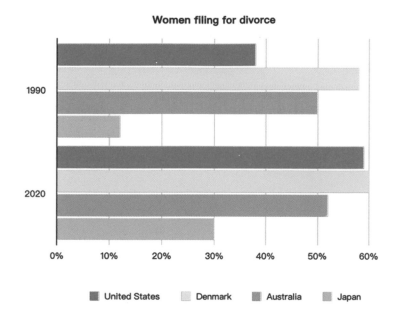

Women filing for divorce

» **…be (almost) the same as/…be (almost) identical to…**

語塊	例句
…be the same as…	The percentage of women filing for divorce in Australia in 1990 **was** almost **the same as** the percentage of women filing for divorce in Australia in 2020.
	■ 比較的兩個主詞相同時（底線）可以用「代名詞」避免重複，如下：
	The percentage of women filing for divorce in Australia in 1990 **was** almost **the same as that** in 2020, **at** approximately 50%.
	（1990 年澳洲婦女申請離婚的比例和 2020 年的幾乎相同，約 50%）
	■ 原句要加上 …at 加上固定數值來讓描述更加具體

…be identical to…	The percentage of women filing for divorce in Australia in 1990 **was** almost **identical to** the percentage of women filing for divorce in Australia in 2020.
	■ 比較的兩個主詞相同時（底線）可以用「代名詞」避免重複，如下：
	The percentage of women filing for divorce in Australia in 1990 **was** almost **identical to that** in 2020, **at** approximately 50%.
	（1990 年澳洲婦女申請離婚的比例和 2020 年的幾乎相同，約 50%）
	■ 原句要加上⋯at 加上固定數值來讓描述更加具體

» **…be similar to…**

語塊	例句
…be similar to…	The percentage of women filing for divorce in the United States in 2020 was similar to the percentage of women filing for divorce in Denmark in 2020.
	■ 比較的兩個主詞相同時（底線）可以用「代名詞」避免重複，但這裡是主題相同而地點不同，改寫方式如下：
	The percentage of women filing for divorce in the United States in 2020 was similar to **that of/ in Denmark** in 2020, **at** about 60%.
	（在 2020 年，美國婦女申請離婚的比例和丹麥的類似，約 60%。）
	■ 原句要加上 …at 加上固定數值來讓描述更加具體

resemble, parallel, correspond
（描述相同處的動詞）

　　本節介紹用來描述長條圖中的三個動詞，內容將會釐清基本定義、熟悉語塊以及使用代名來避免重複。

基本定義

resemble (v)	to look like or be similar to something/someone
parallel (v)	to be similar to something
correspond (v)	to be very similar to or the same as something else

以上定義中的底線內容能幫助我們整理出以下重點：
只有 resemble ＝能用來比較人或事物，剩下的都只能用來比較事物
相似度：resemble = parallel < correspond

✎ 參考圖表

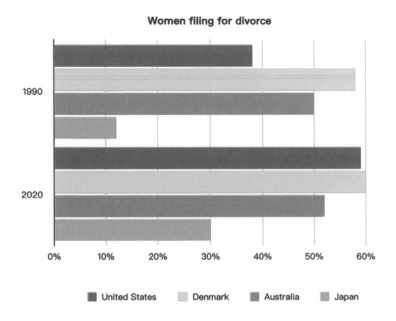

Women filing for divorce

■ United States　■ Denmark　■ Australia　■ Japan

» **A resemble B.**

用法	例句
A resemble B ■ 按情況調整時態 ■ 用來比較人或事	The percentage of women filing for divorce in Australia in 1990 **resembled** the percentage of women filing for divorce in Australia in 2020. ■ 比較的兩個主詞相同時（底線）可以用「代名詞」避免重複，如下： The percentage of women filing for divorce in Australia in 1990 **resembled that** in 2020**, at** approximately 50%. （1990 年澳洲婦女申請離婚的比例與 2020 年的類似，約 50%。） ■ 原句要加上 ...at 加上固定數值來讓描述更加具體

» **A parallel B.**

用法	例句
A parallel B ■ 按情況調整時態 ■ 用來比較事	The percentage of women filing for divorce in Australia in 1990 **paralleled** the percentage of women filing for divorce in Australia in 2020. ■ 比較的兩個主詞相同時（底線）可以用「代名詞」避免重複，如下： The percentage of women filing for divorce in Australia in 1990 **paralleled that** in 2020**, at** approximately 50%. （1990 年澳洲婦女申請離婚的比例與 2020 年的類似，約 50%。） ■ 原句要加上 …at 加上固定數值來讓描述更加具體

» **A correspond to B.**

用法	例句
A correspond to B ■ 不及物動詞，因此其後要加上 to ■ 按狀況調整時態 ■ 用來比較事物	The percentage of women filing for divorce in the United States in 2020 almost corresponded to the percentage of women filing for divorce in Denmark in 2020. ■ 比較的兩個主詞相同時（底線）可以用「代名詞」避免重複，但這裡是主題相同而地點不同，改寫方式如下： The percentage of women filing for divorce in the United States in 2020 almost **corresponded to that of/in** Denmark in 2020**, at** about 60%. （在 2020 年，美國婦女申請離婚的比例和丹麥的相似，約 60%。） ■ 原句要加上 …at 加上固定數值來讓描述更加具體

superior, inferior
（描述相異處的形容詞）

　　本節說明長條圖中用來描述相異處的兩個形容詞，學習內容包過釐清基本定義、熟悉語塊、以及使用代名詞來避免重複。

☞ 基本定義

superior (adj)	greater in quantity or numbers
inferior (adj)	lower in quantity or numbers

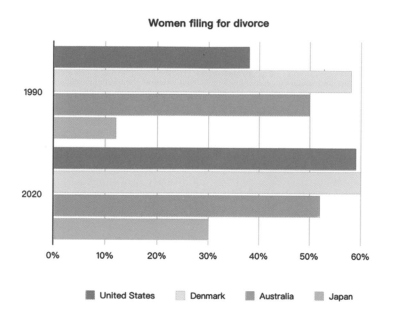

Women filing for divorce

■ United States　□ Denmark　■ Australia　■ Japan

» **…be superior to…**

語塊	例句
…be superior to…（高於）	The percentage of women filing for divorce in Denmark in 1990 **was superior to** the percentage of women filing for divorce in **the United States** in 1990.
	■ 比較的兩個主詞相同時（底線）可以用「代名詞」避免重複，但這裡是主題相同而地點不同，改寫方式如下：
	The percentage of women filing for divorce in Denmark in 1990 **was superior to that of/in** the United States in 1990 **by** about 20%.
	（在 1990 年，丹麥婦女申請離婚的比例比美國高約 20%。）
	■ 原句要加上 …by 加上差距來讓描述更加具體

» **…be inferior to…**

語塊	例句
…be inferior to…（低於）	The percentage of women filing for divorce in Japan in 2020 **was inferior to** the percentage of women filing for divorce in Australia in 2020. ■ 比較的兩個主詞相同時（底線）可以用「代名詞」避免重複，但這裡是主題相同而地點不同，改寫方式如下： The percentage of women filing for divorce in Japan in 2020 **was inferior to that of/in** Australia in 2020 **by** approximately 22%. （在 2020 年，日本婦女申請離婚的比例比澳洲低約 22%。） ■ 原句要加上 …by 加上差距來讓描述更加具體

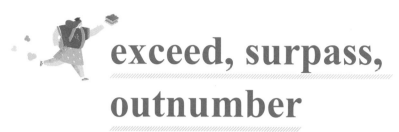

exceed, surpass, outnumber

（描述相異處的動詞）

　　本節說明長條圖中用來描述相異處的三個動詞，學習內容包過釐清基本定義、熟悉語塊、以及使用代名詞來避免重複。

基本定義

surpass (v)	to <u>be even better or greater than</u> someone or something else
exceed (v)	to <u>be more than</u> a particular number or amount
outnumber (v)	to <u>be more in number than</u> another group

按照定義中底線中的內容可以排出這三個動詞的「超出程度」：
surpass > exceed = outnumber

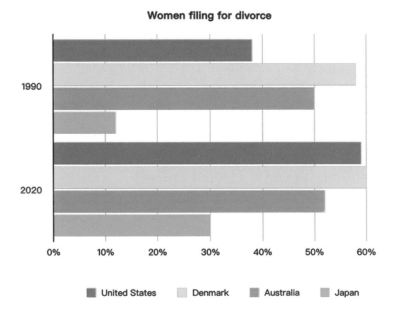

Women filing for divorce

» **A surpass B.**

用法	例句
A surpass B. ■ 按照狀況調整時態 ■ 差距大於約 50% 時用	<u>The percentage of women filing for divorce</u> in Denmark in 2020 surpassed <u>the percentage of women filing for divorce</u> in Japan in 1990. ■ 比較的兩個主詞相同時（底線）可以用「代名詞」避免重複，但這裡是主題相同而地點不同，改寫方式如下： The percentage of women filing for divorce in Denmarkin 2020 surpassed **that of/in** Japanin 1990 **by**approximately 48%. （2020 年丹麥婦女申請離婚的比例比 1990 年日本的超出約 48%。） ■ 原句要加上 ...by 加上差距來讓描述更加具體

» **A exceed B.**

用法	例句
A exceed B. ■ 按照狀況調整時態 ■ 差距不約小於 50% 時用	The percentage of women filing for divorce in Australia in 2020 exceeded the percentage of women filing for divorce in the United States in 1990. ■ 比較的兩個主詞相同時（底線）可以用「代名詞」避免重複，但這裡是主題相同而地點不同，改寫方式如下： The percentage of women filing for divorce in Australia in 2020 **exceeded that of/in** the United States in 1990 **by** about14%. （2020 年澳洲婦女申請離婚的比例比 1990 年美國的多約 14%。） ■ 原句要加上 …by 加上差距來讓描述更加具體

» **A outnumber B.**

用法	例句
A outnumber B. ■ 按照狀況調整時態 ■ 差距小於 50% 時用	The percentage of women filing for divorce in Japan in 2020 outnumbered the percentage of women filing for divorce in 1990. ■ 比較的兩個主詞相同時（底線）可以用「代名詞」避免重複，如下： The percentage of women filing for divorce in Japan in 2020 outnumbered **that** in 1990 by approximately 18%. （2020 年日本婦女申請離婚的比例比 1990 年的多約 18%。） ■ 原句要加上 …by 加上差距來讓描述更加具體

likewise, conversely, ...with the former and the latter

（描述異同的副詞和句型）

本節講解兩個用來描述長條圖中異同的副詞及一個句型，內容包括基本定義、標點符號以及語塊和先前教學內容的應用。

👆 基本定義

likewise (adv)	in the same way
conversely (adv)	used when one situation is the opposite of another
the former (n)	the first of two people or things that you have just mentioned
the latter (n)	the second of two people or things that you have just mentioned

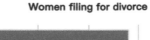 參考圖表

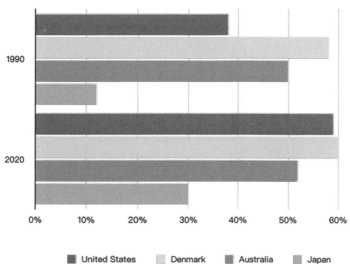

Women filing for divorce

United States　Denmark　Australia　Japan

» 描述相同點：**likewise**

使用	例句
■ S + V. Likewise, S + V. ■ S +V; likewise, S +V.	The percentage of women filing for divorce in Denmark in 2020 was at about 60%. Likewise, the percentage of women filing for divorce in the United States in 1990 was at about 60%. 上述句子能根據以下幾點來修改得更好： ■ 比較的主詞的主題相同但地點不同時，能使用代名詞避免重複 ■ 估算的副詞也能用同義詞避免重複 改後的句如下： The percentage of women filing for divorce in Denmark in 2020 was at **about** 60%. Likewise, **that of/in** the United States in 1990 wat at **approximately** 60%. （2020 年丹麥申請離婚婦女的比例約是 60%。相同地，1990 年美國婦女比例也約是 60%。）

» 描述相異點：conversely

使用	例句
■ S + V. Conversely, S + V. ■ S +V; conversely, S +V.	The percentage of women filing for divorce in Denmark in 2020 was at 60%; conversely, the percentage of women filing for divorce in Japan was at 30% in 2020. 上述句子能根據以下幾點來修改得更好： ■ 比較的主詞的主題相同但地點不同時，能使用代名詞避免重複 改後的句如下： The percentage of women filing for divorce in Denmark in 2020 was at 60%; conversely, that of/in Japan was at 30% in 2020. （2020 年丹麥婦女申請離婚的比例是 60%。相反地，同年 2020 年日本的比例是 30%。）

» 描述同異：S + V, with the former…and the latter.

相同	
使用	例句
■ A be similar to/identical to B, with the former at…and the latter at…	In 2020, the percentage of women filing for divorce in Denmark **was almost identical to that of/in** the United States, **with the former at** 60% **and the latter at** 58%. （在 2020 年，丹麥婦女申請離婚的比例和美國的幾乎相同，前者為 60% 而後者為 58%。）
■ A resemble/parallel/ correspond to B, with the former at…and the latter at…	In 2020, the percentage of women filing for divorce in Denmark **almost corresponded to that of/in** the United States, **with the former at** 60% **and the latter at** 58%. （在 2020 年，丹麥婦女申請離婚的比例和美國的幾乎相同，前者為 60% 而後者為 58%。）

相異	
使用	例句
■ A be superior/inferior to B, with the former at… and the latter at…	The percentage of women filing for divorce in Denmark in 2020 **was superior to that of/in** Japan in 1990, **with the former at** 60% **and the latter at** 12%. （2020 年丹麥申請離婚的婦女比例超過 1990 年日本的，前者為 60% 而後者為 12%。）
■ A surpass/exceed/ outnumber B, with the former at…and the latter at…	The percentage of women filing for divorce in Denmark **surpassed that of/in** Japan in 1990, **with the former at** 60% **and the latter at** 12%. （2020 年丹麥申請離婚的婦女比例超過 1990 年日本的，前者為 60% 而後者為 12%。）

圓 餅 圖

percent vs. percentage

本節說明 percent 及 percentage 的使用，學習內容包括基本定義、分辨方式以及使用上常見的錯誤。

基本定義

percent (n)	one part in a hundred
percentage (n)	an amount of something

🏆 分辨方式

上述定義說明 percent 與數值有關而 percentage 代表的是某物整體的量，因此可以得到以下的分辨原則：

■ 有和數據一起使用時，用 percent

e.g., The global car sales grew by 6 percent. （有數據）

■ 沒有和數據一起使用時，用 percentage

e.g., We receive a significant percentage of our students from Taiwan annually.（無數據）

練習

✍ During the Covid-19 pandemic, a large……….of people were in quarantine.

✍ More than 80……….of the students in Taiwan are against corporal punishment.

👆 常見錯誤

當 percent 和 percentage 與名詞一起在一個句子出現時，許多人會不確定到底要用單數或複數動詞。看以下例子來決定在不同狀況中如何判斷：

■ 當 percent 和 percentage 後加上可數複數名詞，要使用複數動詞。

✍ 70 percent of the <u>residents</u> here <u>are</u> married. （可數）

✍ A small percentage of <u>water goes</u> for outdoor use. （不可數）

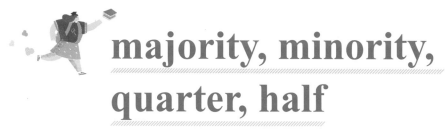

majority, minority, quarter, half
（描述比例的數詞）

本節説明圓餅圖中用來描述比例的「數詞」使用方法，學習內容包括基本定義、搭配句型以及語塊。

👆 基本定義

Majority (n)	Most of the people or things in a group
Minority (n)	A small group of people or things within a much larger group
Quarter (n)	One of four equal parts
Half (n)	One of two equal parts

按以上定義，可將這四個數詞量化	
majority: 大於 50%	minority: 小於 30%
quarter: 25%	half: 50%
註：這些為參考值，要按照實際狀況來使用	

✏ 參考圖表

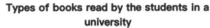

Types of books read by the students in a university

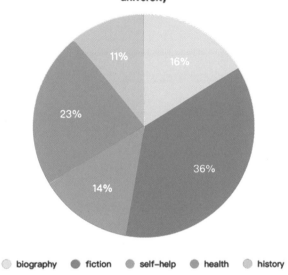

○ biography　● fiction　● self-help　● health　● history

註：無提供時間，使用「現在式」

» Majority

■ A majority of + S + V, at 數值 .	例 A majority of the students read fiction, at 36%. 大多數的學生讀小說，有 36%。
■ A and B beV the majority, at 數值 and 數值 respectively.	例 Fiction and health are the majority, at 36% and 23% respectively. 小說和健康類為多數，依序為 36% 和 23%。

註（一）：圖中沒有類別達到 50%，這時可用比例最高的或前兩高的來描述
註（二）：respectively: in the same order as you have just mentioned（依序地）

» Minority

■ A minority of + S +V, at 數值	例 A minority of the students read history, at 11%. 少數的學生讀歷史類，有 11%。
■ A and B beV the minority, with the former at 數值 and the latter at 數值.	例 History and biography are the minority, with the former at 11% and the latter at 16%. 歷史類和傳記類是少數，前者有 11% 而後者有 16%。
註（一）：圖中有多個低於 50% 的類別時，可以用最低的或前兩低的來描述	
註（二）：…, with the former at…and the latter at…（複習：前者在……而後者在……）	

» Quarter

A quarter of + S +V.	例 About a quarter of the students read health, at 23%. 約有四分之一的學生讀健康類，約 23%。
註：若類別接近 25%，要在 a quarter of 前加上 almost，在後面用 at 標明數據。	

» Half

A half of + S +V.	例 A half of the students read art. 一半的學生讀藝術類。
註：參考圖表中沒有剛好為 50% 的類別，因此以上句子是為了講解而另外寫的例子。	

high, low, small
（描述比例的形容詞）

　　本章說明如何用描述比例的三個形容詞來寫出描述圓餅圖的方式，內容包含基本定義以及與先前教學內容的綜合應用。

👆 基本定義

high (adj)	of greater degree, amount, cost, or value than average
low (adj)	small in number or amount
small (adj)	little or close to zero

由以上定義可以排出比例高低，如下
high (fiction, health) > low (biography, self-help)> small (history)
按狀況選形容詞來描述比例

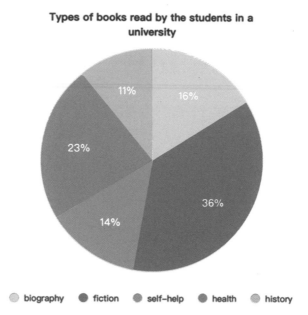

Types of books read by the students in a university

○ biography ● fiction ● self-help ● health ○ history

註：無提供時間，使用「現在式」

» High

■ A high percentage of S + V, at 數值.	例 A high percentage of the students read fiction, at 36%. 高比例的學生讀小說，有 36%。 例 A high percentage of the students read health, at 23%. 高比例的學生讀健康類，有 23%。

註：當 percentage 後加上可數複數名詞，要使用複數動詞。

» Low

■ Alow percentage of S + V, at 數值 .	例 A low percentage of students read biography, at 16%. 低比例的學生讀傳記，有 16%。 例 A low percentage of students read self-help, at 14 %. 低比例的學生讀成長類，有 14%。

註：當 percentage 後加上可數複數名詞，要使用複數動詞。

» Small

■ A low percentage of S + V, at 數值 .	例 A small percentage of students read history, at 11%. 少部分的學生讀歷史，有 11%。

註：當 percentage 後加上可數複數名詞，要使用複數動詞。

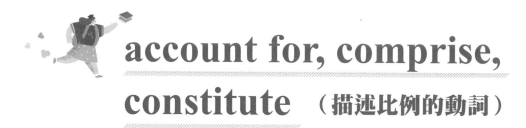

account for, comprise, constitute （描述比例的動詞）

本章講解用來描述圓餅圖比例的三個動詞，內容包含基本定義、使用方式以及與綜合應用。

👆 基本定義

account for (v)	to form a particular amount or part of something
comprise (v)	to form a part of a larger group of people or things
constitute (v)	to form a part of something

由以上定義能得知這三個動詞為同義詞。

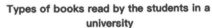

✏️ 參考圖表

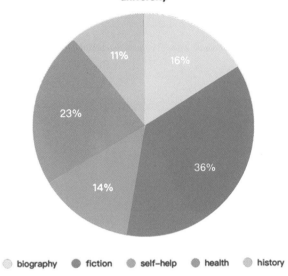

Types of books read by the students in a university

○ biography ● fiction ● self-help ● health ● history

註：無提供時間，使用「現在式」

» **…account for…**

■ S + account for 數值 .	例 Fiction accounts for 36%. 小說佔了 36%。
■ S + account for a high/low/small percentage, at 數值 .	例 Fiction accounts for a high percentage, at 36%. 小說佔了 36%。

» **…comprise…**

■ S + comprise 數值 .	例 Biography comprises 16%. 傳記佔了 16%。
■ S + comprise a high/low/small percentage, at 數值 .	例 Biographycomprises a low percentage, at 16%. 傳記佔了 16%。

» **...constitute...**

■ S + constitute 數值 .	例 History constitutes 11%. 歷史佔了 11%。
■ S + constitute a high/low/small percentage, at 數值 .	例 History comprises a small percentage, at 11%. 歷史佔了 11%。

常用句型

本章介紹在描述圓餅圖時常用的句型，例句整合先前所有的學習內容。

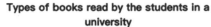
參考圖表

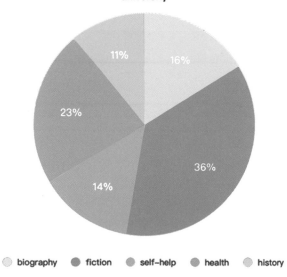

Types of books read by the students in a university

biography	fiction	self-help	health	history

biography 16%, fiction 36%, self-help 14%, history 23%, health 11%

註：無提供時間，使用「現在式」

» 描述主要趨勢

■ S+ beV the most/least common/ popular/prevalent + category/ activity/product.

例 Fiction is the most popular category. 小說是最受歡迎的類別。

註（一）：此處三個形容詞（common, popular, prevalent）都有「普遍」的意思
註（二）：此處的名詞（category, activity, product）視圖表主題選用

» 同級比較與倍數詞

■ A + beV + 倍數 + as much as + B, with the former at 數值 and the latter at 數值.

例 Health is twice as much as history, with the former at 23% and the latter at 11%.
健康類是歷史類的兩倍，前者有 23% 而後者有 11%。

兩倍：twice；N 倍：N times

» 比較級與倍數詞

■ A + beV + 倍數 + more than + B, at 數值 and 數值 respectively.

例 Fiction is three times more than history, at 36% and 11% respectively.
小說是歷史類的三倍，依序為 36% 和 11%。

II

議論寫作

我們一樣能經由評分標準中的「任務達成」和「詞彙資源」的說明獲得「議論寫作」單字準備的方向，下為六級分的敘述：

級分	任務達成	詞彙資源
6	■ 有處理任務的所有面向，但討論的程度不均（addresses all parts of the task although some parts may be more fully covered than others） ■ 呈現一個清楚的立場，但結論不清楚或重複（presents a relevant position although the conclusion may become unclear or repetitive） ■ 呈現相關的要點，但有些發展不全或不清楚（presents relevant main ideas but some may be inadequately developed or unclear）	■ 任務中使用的詞彙範圍廣（uses an adequate range of vocabulary for the task） ■ 嘗試使用較不通俗的字彙但其使用不正確（attempts to use less common vocabulary but with some inaccuracy） ■ 犯下拼字或字型變化的錯誤，但這些錯誤不影響文意（makes some errors in spelling and/or word formation, but they do not impede communication）

以上內容替議論寫作的單字準備列出三大原則：

（一）用字能精準以清楚表達立場；（二）能善用邏輯標記字來舉證說明與承接上下文；（三）不能犯拼字或字型變化的錯誤以免阻礙文意的傳達。

若將這些原則與議論文的各種命題並列，我們能更具體地瞭解學習方向。例如：在處理同意或不同意的命題時，就得知道如何表達對特定言論的認同與否；在面對優劣勢的命題時，就要注意評斷好壞的用詞；在分析問題產生的因

素和提供解決方法時，就必須掌握關於解釋原因和說明解決問題過程的用字。在回答各種命題時也有特定的句型來協助表達，因此考生同樣得熟悉字型變化以符合文法，同時也得知道同義或近義詞來發展段落。

　　議論文指派的議題來自不同領域，因此考生也得學會用來討論各種議題的核心單字，而常見的主題包含學習、科技、人際、健康、與環境等。因此，議論寫作的單字準備要聚焦在熟悉各類命題的用字、懂得根據不同的句構來變化字型和用同義或近義詞銜接文意，以及掌握常見主題的關鍵字。換句話説，議論寫作的單字擴充要以兩個核心來進行—「結構性語塊」與「內容性語塊」。

👆 重要觀念

■ 語塊：字組成的小團體，通常一起使用的字

e.g., …listen to…; …depend on…; …between…and…

■ 結構性語塊：用來銜接、連貫、總結等組織語意用的架構

e.g., To begin with, …; Firstly, …; To sum up, ….

■ 內容性語塊：用來討論不同主題想法的單字

文章主題若為「兒童與玩具」，就有可能用到以下的字：
e.g., hand-eye coordination, attention span, …distract…from

　　接下來的章節會替每種命題提供兩篇範文，從範文中彙整以下學習重點：

內容性語塊 ➡ **結構性語塊** ➡ **大綱**

★ 説明各類主題中重要單字的使用方法

★ 歸納組織文章各段落的架構

★ 整理文章重點來累積對不同議題知識，逐步培養思考與論述能力

同意或不同意（一）

You should spend about 40 minutes on this task.

Some people believe that voluntary community services should be a compulsory part of high school education. To what extent do you agree or disagree?

Give reasons for your answer and include any relevant examples from your own knowledge or experience.

Write at least 250 words.

範文

It is said that students should **partake in** unpaid community services as a **mandatory** part of their curriculum in high schools. I strongly **agree with** this opinion based on several reasons.

To begin with, teenagers can grow **tremendously** through serving the community **freely**. When working **voluntarily**, students learn how to solve unexpected problems without the **instructions** from their teachers and parents. They have the **opportunity** to be more **independent**. In the meantime, teenagers **involved in** community services are able to understand that the **contributions** they make have impacts on others' lives. Therefore, they become much more **motivated** to help and more **responsible for** all the works they are **assigned**.

Secondly, partaking in unpaid community services provides **a myriad of** benefits. If students serve the community freely, especially working for **a charitable foundation**, they will have the opportunity to meet people from different **socioeconomic** backgrounds, many of whom are **orphans**, **disabled** children, or **the elderly** in nursing homes. Meeting these people **develops** their sense of **empathy for** other's destiny. What is more, students come to understand the value of labor much better by performing the work without payment. They have deeper **gratitude towards** what they have. If unpaid community services are made **compulsory** at schools, they will know how difficult it is to complete the work and stop **taking** things for **granted**.

In conclusion, I strongly agree that **participating in** unpaid community services can **be beneficial to** students because it transforms them into mature, responsible, and grateful **individuals**.

☝ 內容性語塊

導論	
partake (vi.) 參加	• **語塊** …partake in…
	例 Students should <u>partake in</u> community services. 學生應該要參加社區服務。
	例 <u>Partaking in</u> community services teaches students valuable lessons. 參與社區服務教學生重要的課題。
mandatory (adj.) 強制的	例 Community services should be <u>a mandatory part</u> in high school education. 社區服務應要強制變成高中教育的一部分。
	例 High schools should make it <u>mandatory for students to</u> partake in community services.

| agree (vi)
同意 | • **語塊 …agree with sb on sth.**

例 All parents <u>agreed with</u> the school <u>on</u> the decision to send all the students to do community services.
全體家長同意學校送所有學生去社區服務的決定。

• **語塊 …agree that 句子**

例 All parents <u>agreed that</u> doing community services should be mandatory at schools.
全體家長同意學校應要讓做社區服務變成強制。

• **語塊 …agree to V…**

例 All parents <u>agreed to</u> send their children to do community services.
全體家長同意讓他們的小孩去做社區服務。 |

正文第一段	
tremendously (adv.) 極大地	例 Community services make students <u>grow tremendously</u>. 社區服務讓學生成長非常多。 例 Community services are <u>tremendously important</u> to all students. 社區服務對所有學生極為重要。
freely (adv.) 無償地	例 Students serve the community <u>freely</u>. 學生無償替服務社區。 例 Students agreed to do community services <u>freely</u>. 學生同意無償替社區服務。
voluntarily (adv.) 自願地	例 Students serve the community <u>voluntarily</u>. 學生自願替社區無償服務。 例 Students agreed to do community services <u>voluntarily</u>. 學生同意自願替社區服務。

instruction (n.) 指導	例 When doing community services, students do not <u>receive any instructions from</u> their teachers or parents. 當學生在做社區服務時，他們不會接受任何來自老師或家長的指導。 例 Teachers and parents cannot <u>give instructions on</u> how these services should be done. 老師和家長無法給有關這些服務該如何做的指令。
opportunity (n.) 機會	• 搭配詞：**...provide/have...the opportunity to...** 例 Doing community services <u>provides students the opportunity</u> to grow. 從事社區服務提供學生能成長的機會。 • 搭配詞：**...a valuable opportunity** 例 Students <u>have a valuable opportunity to</u> help others when partaking in community services. 當學生參與社區服務時，他們有能幫助他人的寶貴機會。
independent (adj) 獨立的	例 Without the instructions from teachers, students can <u>become</u> more <u>independent</u> through community services. 沒有老師的指導，學生能透過社區服務變得更獨立。 例 Making community services mandatory gives students the opportunity to <u>be independent</u>. 使社區服務變成強制給學生一個能變獨立的機會。
involved (adj) 參與的	• 語塊 **...be involved in...** 例 Students who <u>are involved</u> in community services can learn to be more independent. 參與社區服務的學生能學習如何變得獨立。 例 <u>Being involved in</u> community services makes students grow tremendously. 參與社區服務能讓學生成長很多。

contribution (n) 貢獻	• **語塊 …make contributions to…** 例 By being involved in community services, students can make contributions to the society. 透過參與社區服務，學生能為社會帶來貢獻。 例 Students can make significant contributions to the community. 學生能為社會帶來重大的貢獻。
impact (n) 影響	• **語塊 …have an impact on…** 例 Doing community services has an impact on how students understand and look at the society. 從事社區服務對學生瞭解和看待社會的方式有影響。 例 Partaking in community services has a positive impact on students. 參與社區服務對學生有正面的影響。
motivated (adj) 積極的	• **語塊 …be motivated to…** 例 Knowing how serving the community can have a positive impact on the society, students become motivated to make more contributions. 知道從事社區服務是如何對社會有好的影響後，學生變得更積極做貢獻。 例 Students are highly motivated to partake in different tasks. 學生很積極參加不同的任務。
responsible (adj) 負責的	• **語塊 …be responsible for…** 例 Students are responsible for a variety of tasks. 學生要為各式各樣的任務負責。 例 By being responsible for different tasks, students are more independent. 藉由對不同任務負責，學生更獨立了。

assign (v) 指派	• **語塊 …assign sb to…** 例 Schools should <u>assign students to</u> do community service. 學校應要指派學生去做社區服務。 • **語塊 …be assigned to…** 例 Students <u>are assigned to</u> finish tasks completely different from those at school. 學生被指派去做和學校完全不同的任務。

正文第二段

myriad (n.) 無數	• **語塊 …a myriad of…** 例 Students have the opportunity to complete <u>a myriad of</u> tasks they have never been assigned at school. 學生有機會能完成無數他們在學校沒被指派過的任務。 例 Partaking in <u>a myriad of</u> community services, students become more responsible for others and themselves. 參與無數的社區服務後，學生變得更加為他人和自己負責。
charitable foundation (n.) 慈善機構	例 These students have helped multiple <u>charitable foundations</u> voluntarily over the summer. 這些學生已在夏季時自願幫助無數個慈善機構。 例 All students involved in the <u>charitable foundation</u> know that their contributions have a positive impact on others. 全體參與慈善機構的學生都知道他們的貢獻對其他人有正面的影響。

socioeconomic (adj.) 社經的	例 Doing community services allows students to know people from different socioeconomic backgrounds. 做社區服務能讓學生認識來自不同社經背景的人。
	例 Being assigned a myriad of tasks, students become not merely more responsible but also more aware of the needs of different socioeconomic groups. 被指派無數任務後，學生變得不僅更負責也更瞭解不同社經團體的需求。
orphan (n.) 孤兒	例 Students are sometimes assigned to accompany orphans. 學生有時會被派去陪伴孤兒。
	例 Accompanying orphans gives students the opportunity to learn more about people from a completely socioeconomic group of their own. 陪伴孤兒給學生機會認識來自與自己不同社經團體的人們。
disabled (adj.) 失能的 elderly (adj.) 年老的	• **"the + adj"：泛指一群特殊的人；複數** **e.g., the disabled, the elderly** 例 Students are responsible for taking care of the disabled and the elderly in the charitable foundation. 學生在慈善機構裡要負責照顧失能與年老的人們。
	例 Seeing how the lives of the disabled and the elderly are improved, students are even more motivated to make other contributions. 看到失能和年老人們的生活被改善後，學生變得更加積極去做其他貢獻。
develop (v.) 開發；養成	• **語塊 …develop a sense of…** 例 Partaking in community services helps students develop a sense of responsibility. 參與社區服務幫助學生養成責任感。
	例 By completing different tasks, students develop a myriad of skills they can use in the future. 藉由完成不同的任務，學生開發無數他們未來能用的技能。

empathy (n.) 同情	• **語塊 …have empathy for…** 例 Meeting the less fortunate in different charitable foundations enables students to have empathy for other's destiny. 在不同慈善團體見到較不幸的人們使學生能夠同情他人的命運。 例 When students develop empathy for others, they can grow tremendously. 當學生養成對他人的同情，他們就能成長許多。
gratitude (n.) 感激	• **語塊 …have gratitude towards…** 例 After completing a myriad of tasks in the charitable foundation, all students have gratitude towards their parents. 在慈善機構完成無數的任務後，全體學生都對他們的父母感到感激。 例 Having gratitude towards others is what students cannot learn from the instructions at school. 對他人感到感激是無法從學校的指導學會的。
compulsory (adj.) 強制的	例 Knowing the positive impacts community service can have on their children, most parents agree with making it compulsory at school. 瞭解社區服務如何對他們的小孩有正面影響後，多數的家長同意讓它在學校變成強制。 例 Compulsory community service gives students the chance to help people from different socioeconomic backgrounds. 強制的社區服務給學生機會去幫助來自不同社經背景的人們。

take…for granted (v) 視……為理所當然	例 Without partaking in community services, students tend to <u>take</u> everything <u>for granted</u>. 沒有參加社區服務的話，學生傾向把所有事情視為理所當然。
	例 Through meeting and helping people from different socioeconomic groups in the charitable foundation, students stopped <u>taking</u> everything <u>for granted</u>. 由見到和幫助在慈善機構來自不同社經團體的人們，學生不再視所有事情為理所當然。

結論

participate (vi.) 參加	• **語塊 …participate in…** 例 Students should <u>participate in</u> community services. 學生應該要參加社區服務。 例 <u>Participating in</u> community services teaches students valuable lessons. 參與社區服務教學生重要的課題。
beneficial (adj.) 有益的	• **語塊 …be beneficial to…** 例 Participating in community services <u>is beneficial to</u> students because it teaches them a myriad of skills. 參加社區服務對學生有益因為它能教他們無數的技能。 例 Helping people from different socioeconomic backgrounds <u>is beneficial to</u> society. 幫助來自不同社經背景的人們對社會有益。
individual (n.) 個人	例 Community services transform students into mature, responsible, and grateful <u>individuals</u>. 社區服務讓學生變成成熟、負責和懂得感恩的人們。 例 Students are assigned to help <u>individuals</u> with different needs. 學生被派去幫助有不同需求的人們。

🏆 結構性語塊

導論	■ **表達立場：S agree with…based on…reasons.** e.g., **I strongly** agree with **this opinion based on several reasons**.
正文第一段	■ **提出第一個理由：To begin with,…** e.g., To begin with, teenagers can grow tremendously through serving the community freely. ■ **提出第一個例子：When V-ing, S + V.** e.g., When working voluntarily, students learn how to solve unexpected problems without the instructions from their teachers and parents. ■ **提出第二個例子：In the meantime, S + V.** e.g., In the meantime, teenagers involved in community services are able to understand that the contributions they make have impacts on others' lives. ■ **收尾：Therefore, S + V.** e.g., Therefore, they become much more motivated to help and more responsible for all the works they are assigned.

正文第二段	■ 提出第二個理由：**Secondly, S + V.** e.g., Secondly, partaking in unpaid community services provides a myriad of benefits. ■ 提出第一個例子：**If S + V, S + V.** e.g., If students serve the community freely, especially working for a charitable foundation, they will have the opportunity to meet people from different socioeconomic backgrounds… ■ 提出第二個例子：**What is more, S + V.** e.g., What is more, students come to understand the value of labor much better by performing the work without payment. ■ 收尾：**If S + V, S +V.** e.g., If unpaid community services are made compulsory at schools, they will know how difficult it is to complete the work and stop taking things for granted.
結論	■ 總結：**In conclusion, S + V.** e.g., In conclusion, I strongly agree that participating in unpaid community services can be beneficial to students….

👆 文章大綱

正文第一段	正文第二段
II. Teenagers can grow tremendously. 　A. They learn how to solve problems. 　B. They understand that their contributions have impacts. 　C. They become more motivated and responsible.	III. Community services give students a myriad of benefits. 　A. They meet people from different socioeconomic backgrounds. 　B. They develop empathy for others. 　C. They have gratitude for what they have.

同意或不同意（二）

You should spend about 40 minutes on this task.

When choosing a job, salary is the most important consideration. To what extent do you agree or disagree?

Give reasons for your answer and include any relevant examples from your own knowledge or experience.

Write at least 250 words.

 範文

It is true that salary plays an **integral** part in choosing a job. However, I **disagree** with making it a top **priority** because there are other factors that should be put into **consideration**.

Most people consider salary the most **crucial** factor when choosing a job for different reasons. Some believe that income is **proportional** to the quality of life. The higher you earn, the better you live. They can afford their increasing demand on not only basic needs but also luxuries, such as fashion or holidays. Other people **regard** salary as a measure of their success in the workplace. The higher income they receive, the more valuable they are. Thus, salary is **front and center** for many because it might lead to a better life and career **prospect**.

On the other hand, more and more people are paying **attention** to other factors. First, many job seekers **emphasize** a healthy **work-life balance**. Even if their positions offer **competitive** salary, they still cannot stand working long hours in front of the computer every day, leaving no room for freedom and other leisure activities. In the meantime, people start choosing jobs that contribute to the society. For instance, some go to rural areas to **assist** and improve the performance of local **enterprises instead of** working for **well-established** companies. Although they are not paid as much, they are satisfied with their choices because they help increase the average income of the local residents. Clearly, these factors bring people a much stronger sense of satisfaction than salary.

In conclusion, it is true that salary matters. Yet, it is **by no means** the key consideration people should **attend** to when making a career decision.

☞ 內容性語塊

導論	
integral (adj.) 構成所必須的	• 語塊 **…play an integral role in…** 例 Salary <u>plays an integral role in</u> choosing a job. 薪資是選工作時必須考量的事項。 • 語塊 **…be integral to…** 例 Freedom and leisure activities <u>are integral to</u> good health. 自由和休閒活動對健康來説是不可獲缺的。
disagree (vi.) 不同意	• 語塊 **…disagree with sb. on sth…** 例 I <u>disagree with</u> my parents <u>on</u> salary being the most important factor in choosing a job. 我不同意我父母説薪資是選工作時最重要的因素。 • 語塊 **…disagree that…** 例 I <u>disagree that</u> salary is the most important factor in choosing a job. 我不同意薪資是選工作時最重要的因素。

priority (n.) 優先	• 語塊 …take priority over… 例 When it comes to choosing a job, salary shouldn't take priority over work environment. 說到選工作，薪資不應比工作環境重要。 • 搭配詞 …a first/top/low priority 例 Some people disagree that salary is a top priority in choosing a job. 有些人不同意薪水在選工作時應是最高優先。
consideration (n.) 考量	• 語塊 …put…into consideration 例 To choose a job properly, people should put different factors into consideration. 為了要好好選一份工作，人們應要把不同的因素納入考量。 • 搭配詞 …deserve consideration 例 In addition to salary, other factors deserve consideration in making a career choice. 除了薪水，在選工作時，其他因素也應被考量。

正文第一段

crucial (adj.) 非常重要的	• 語塊 …be crucial to… 例 High income is crucial to the quality of life. 高薪對生活品質非常重要。 • 語塊 …be crucial in… 例 Having a job that makes contributions to the society is crucial in my career plan. 擁有一份能為社會貢獻的工作在我的職涯規劃中非常重要。

proportional (adj.) 與……成比例的	• **語塊** …be proportional to… 例 Some believe that income is proportional to the quality of life. 有些人相信薪水和生活品質成比例。 例 Others consider how much you earn might not necessarily be proportional to how happy you are. 其他人認為你賺多少錢不盡然和你多快樂成比例。
regard (v.) 將……認為	• **語塊** …regard…as… 例 People tend to regard salary as a measure of their success in the workplace. 人們傾向視薪水為衡量他們在職場成就的依據。 例 Some parents regard high income as an integral part of a good life. 有些父母視高薪為好生活不可或缺的一部分。
front and center (adj.) 核心的；重要的	例 For those who pursue a sense of achievement in life, making contributions to the society should be front and center in their jobs. 對那些在人生中追求成就感的人，貢獻社會是他們工作的核心。 例 For those who contribute to the society, salary might not be front and center. 對那些為社會貢獻的人，薪水並沒那麼重要。
prospect (n.) 前景	例 A lot of people firmly believe that the higher the income, the better the prospect in life. 許多人深信薪水越高，人生的前景就越好。 例 Experience and skills are integral to an individual's career prospect. 經驗和技能對一個人工作前景是不可或缺的。

正文第二段	
attention (n.) 注意	• **語塊 …pay attention to…** 例 More and more job seekers are <u>paying attention to</u> other factors, such as work environment. 越來越多的求職者開始注意其他的因素，像是工作環境。 • **語塊 …draw attention to…** 例 In the discussion with my parents, they <u>drew attention to</u> the importance of getting a job that contributes to the society. 在我與父母的討論中，他們強調要找到一份能對社會有貢獻的工作的重要性。
emphasize (v.) 強調	• **正確：emphasize + O；錯誤：emphasize on** 例 They always <u>emphasize</u> the importance of work environment. 他們總是強調工作環境的重要性。 • **語塊…emphasize that/how…** 例 They always <u>emphasize how</u> important work environment is. 他們總是強調工作環境是多麼的重要。
work-life balance (n.) 工作與生活間的平衡	• **搭配詞：have a work-life balance** 例 When it comes to choosing a job, <u>having a work-life balance</u> should be front and center. 提到在選工作時，擁有工作與生活間的平衡相當重要。 例 It is unwise to earn more money at the price of losing a <u>work-life balance</u>. 為了賺更多錢而犧牲了工作與生活間的平衡很不明智。

competitive (adj.) 具有競爭力的（價格、服務）	例 Looking into the industry you are interested in helps you confirm whether a company offers you a competitive salary. 調查你有興趣的產業能幫助你確認這間公司是否給你具有競爭力的薪水。 例 If your company doesn't offer you a competitive salary, start looking for a new job. 如果你的公司沒有提供你具有競爭力的薪水，開始找一份新工作吧！
assist (v.) 協助	• **語塊 …assist sb. with sth…** 例 Consulting career advisers assists people with making a sound decision in finding a job. 諮詢職涯顧問協助人們在找工作時做出明智的決定。 • **語塊 …assist sb to…** 例 My career advisor assisted me to weigh my options carefully. 我的職涯顧問幫助我仔細衡量我的選擇。
enterprise (n.) 企業	例 Some go to rural areas to assist and improve the performance of local enterprises instead of working in well-known companies. 有些人去偏遠地區協助和改善在地企業而非替知名公司工作。 例 My sense of satisfaction is in proportion to how much the local enterprise I work with grows. 我的滿足感和我合作的在地企業成長多少成比例。
well-established (adj.) 公認的；廣為人知的	例 Working for a well-established company is integral to my success in the workplace. 替廣為人知的公司工作對我在職場的成功不可或缺。 例 Most people regard working for a well-established enterprise a stepping stone to success and wealth. 許多人視替一間廣為人知的公司工作為成功和財富的墊腳石。

結論	
by no means (adv.) 絕不；一點都不	例 High income is by no means the key factor in choosing a job. 高薪絕不是在選工作時的關鍵因素。 例 Knowing how much my job can contribute to the society, I am convinced that salary is by no means a top priority. 知道我的工作能對社會供獻多少後，我相信薪水絕不會是最高優先。
attend (v.) 注意	• 語塊 …attend to… 例 A proper work-life balance is what you should attend to when making a career decision. 適當的工作與生活間的平衡是你在做職涯決定時要注意的。 例 More and more job seekers are attending to other factors, such as work environment. 越來越多的求職者開始注意其他的因素，像是工作環境。

☝ 結構性語塊

導論

■ 表達立場：I disagree with…because there are other factors that should be put into consideration.

e.g., I disagree with **making it a top priority** because there are other factors that should be put into consideration.

正文第一段	■ 說明一個面向：Most people consider…when V-ing for different reasons. e.g., **Most people consider** salary the most crucial factor **when** choosing a job **for different reasons**. ■ 提出第一個例子：Some people believe that… e.g., **Some believe that** income is proportional to the quality of life. ■ 提出第二個例子：Other people regard…as… e.g., **Other people regard** salary **as** a measure of their success in the workplace. ■ 收尾：Thus, S + V. e.g., **Thus**, salary is front and center for many because it might lead to a better life and career prospect.
正文第二段	■ 說明另一個面向：On the other hand, more and more people… e.g., **On the other hand, more and more people** are paying attention to other factors. ■ 提出第一個例子：First, S + V. e.g., **First**, many job seekers emphasize a healthy work-life balance. ■ 提出第二個例子：In the meantime, S + V. e.g., **In the meantime**, people start choosing jobs that contribute to the society. ■ 收尾：Clearly, S +V. e.g., **Clearly**, these factors bring people a much stronger sense of satisfaction than salary.

結論	■ 總結先讓步：In conclusion, it is true that…
	e.g., **In conclusion, it is true that** salary matters.
	■ 再重申立場：Yet, it is…
	e.g., **Yet, it is** by no means the key consideration people should attend to when making a career decision.

大綱

正文第一段	正文第二段
II. People think salary is the most important factor when they choose a job for different reasons. 　A. Income is proportional to the quality of life. 　B. People think salary represents their success in the workplace.	III. More and more people pay attention to other factors. 　A. They emphasize a healthy work-life balance. 　B. They start to choose jobs that contribute to the society.

優劣勢（一）

You should spend about 40 minutes on this task.

Young people are often influenced by others in the same age. This is called 'peer pressure.' Do the advantages of having peer pressure outweigh the disadvantages?

Give reasons for your answer and include any relevant examples from your own knowledge or experience.

Write at least 250 words.

範文

It is **undeniable** that the effects of peer pressure on youngsters have been **debated heatedly**. As far as I am concerned, the **advantages** of having peer pressure **outweigh** the **disadvantages**.

On the one hand, peer pressure can bring massive advantages to youngsters. Firstly, peer pressure is able to help young people **blend** into the new community more easily. Through meeting others with similar **characteristics** and hobbies, youngsters gain **a sense of belonging**. Secondly, it can **boost cooperation** and **solidarity** among students in learning through teamwork and discussions. Lastly, by **endeavoring** to not merely improve themselves but also achieve their ambitions with peers, the young's **determination** becomes much greater. They are driven to complete tasks together in spite of the **hurdles** ahead of them.

On the other hand, peer pressure results in some **adverse demerits. Inevitably,** surrounded by their peers, youngsters are likely to become envious and start **allocating** their time and money in order to keep up with their friends. For instance, some students might **squander** their tuition on buying handbags to stay fashionable and popular on campus. In addition, students might be afraid of expressing personality traits genuinely in groups for fear that they might be excluded by their friends. They are pressured to **conform** to others to keep their friendship **intact**.

In conclusion, peer pressure certainly poses negative impacts on teenagers to some extent. However, it can still be beneficial as long as it is **harnessed** properly. Therefore, youngsters should be aware of how to take advantage of peer pressure to make it a driving force for **self-actualization**.

☝ 內容性語塊

導論	
undeniable (adj.) 不可否認的	📖 It is an undeniable fact that peer pressure influences youngsters significantly. 同儕壓力明顯影響年輕人是不可否認的事實。 📖 The influence of peer pressure on youngsters is undeniable. 同儕壓力對年輕人的影響是不可否認的。

debate (v.) 爭論	• **語塊 …debate whether/how/what…** 例 Parents and teachers alike have <u>debated whether</u> peer pressure is detrimental to teenagers for years. 不論家長或老師已爭論同儕壓力使否對青少年有害好多年了。 • **語塊 …debate with sb.** 例 Parents have <u>debated with</u> teachers on the impact of peer pressure. 家長和老師爭論同儕壓力的影響。
heatedly (adv.) 激烈地	例 Some teenagers stay quiet in a friendship group to avoid arguing <u>heatedly</u> with others. 有些青少年在朋友圈中保持沈默為了避免和他人激烈地爭論。 例 Psychologists have argued <u>heatedly</u> how peer pressure can be positive in the emotional development of teenagers. 心理學家有激烈地爭論同儕壓力如何能對青年的心理發展有正面的影響。
advantage (n.) 優勢	• **搭配詞 a big/great/massive advantage** 例 Being observant gives you <u>a massive advantage</u> in a new environment as you are able to tell who the difficult people are fast. 懂得察言觀色能在新環境中給你一大優勢因為你能快速地辨識難搞的人是哪些。 • **搭配詞 work to sb's advantage** 例 Peer pressure can <u>work to your advantage</u> if you know how to tell right from wrong. 若你能分辨是非，同儕壓力能對你有利。

outweigh (v.) 大於；比…… 重要	例 The advantages of peer pressure far <u>outweigh</u> the disadvantages. 同儕壓力的優勢大於劣勢。 例 The benefits of collaborating with others <u>outweigh</u> any possible setbacks. 與他人合作的好處大於任何潛在的障礙。
disadvantages (n.) 劣勢	• **語塊 …at a disadvantage** 例 The new student is <u>at a disadvantage</u> in class because he barely knows anyone. 這新學生在班上處於劣勢因為他幾乎不認識任何人。 • **搭配詞 …put/place…at a disadvantage** 例 If you don't exercise moderate judgement when taking your friend's advice, you may <u>put yourself at a disadvantage</u>. 如果你在接受友人建議時不適當地做評斷，你有可能把自己放入劣勢中。

正文第一段

blend (v.) 融入	• **語塊 …blend into…** 例 When attending a new school, some students might have trouble <u>blending into</u> others. 當學生去新學校時，有些可能會在融入他人上遇到麻煩 • **語塊 …blend with…** 例 Peer pressure sometimes compels students to <u>blend fast with</u> their surroundings. 同儕壓力有時會迫使學生快速融入環境。

characteristic (n.) 特色	• **搭配詞 a common characteristic** 例 Teenagers have <u>common characteristics</u>, such as being unwilling to take advice from teachers and parents. 青少年有共同的特質，像是不願意接受老師和父母的建議。
	• **搭配詞 …share a characteristic** 例 Youngsters <u>share a characteristic</u> – they are influenced by peer pressure easily. 年輕人共有一個特質 ── 他們很容易受同儕影響。
a sense of belonging (n.) 歸屬感	• **補充 a sense of achievement（成就感）；a sense of humor（幽默感）** 例 Generally, students try their best to fit in at school to have <u>a sense of belonging</u>. 普遍來看，學生盡力融入學校來得到歸屬感。 例 If students don't have <u>a sense of belonging</u> in their classroom, they might feel less motivated to go to school. 如果學生在教室中沒有歸屬感，他們可能就不太想去上學。
boost (v.) 提高	• **搭配詞 boost sb's confidence** 例 Completing school projects successfully with friends <u>boosts students' confidence</u> in learning. 與朋友成功地完成學校課業提高學生對學習的信心。 例 Peer pressure sometimes <u>boosts</u> the academic performance of students. 同儕壓力有時能提高學生的學業表現。

cooperation (n.) 合作	• **語塊** …cooperation with…
	例 Students understand how they communicate with others better through the cooperation with their peers. 學生透過與同儕合作能更瞭解自己如何與他人溝通。
	• **搭配詞** active/effective cooperation
	例 Effective cooperation is rewarding not merely for the individual but also the group. 有效的合作不僅讓個人也讓整個團隊感到有收穫。
solidarity (n.) 團結	• **搭配詞** demonstrate sb's solidarity
	例 Teenagers generally don't turn their friends down in order to demonstrate their solidarity. 青少年通常不會拒絕朋友以展現團結。
	例 Some teenagers find it stressful to demonstrate their solidarity with their friends. 有些青少年覺得對朋友展現團結感到壓力。
endeavor (v.) 努力去……	• **語塊** …endeavor to…
	例 The majority of the students endeavor to blend into others to have a sense of belonging at school. 多數的學生努力融入他人以在學校獲得歸屬感。
	例 Students endeavor to boost their performance more efficiently through active cooperation with others. 學生透過積極與他人合作來有效地提升他們的表現。
determination (n.) 決心	例 By endeavoring to not merely improve themselves but also achieve their ambitions with peers, the young's determination becomes much greater. 藉由和同儕一起努力去精進自己和達到目標，年輕人的決定變得更強大。
	例 These students showed their determination to win when they debated heatedly with their teammates. 這些學生在他們激烈地與隊員爭論時展現了他們要贏的決心。

driven (adj.) 奮發努力的	例 Students become much more <u>driven</u> to accomplish anything when working with their peers. 當學生和同儕合作時，他們變得更加努力去完成任何事。 例 Students might not be <u>driven</u> to learn when not blending in others. 當學生沒有融入他人時，他們或許會不想努力去學習。
hurdle (n.) 障礙	例 Peer pressure can be a <u>hurdle</u> for some students at school. 同儕壓力對一些學生來說是一個在學校的障礙。 例 Students should be taught how to handle peer pressure so as to clear all the <u>hurdles</u> in interpersonal relationship. 學生應被教導如何處理同儕壓力以清除所有在人際關係上的障礙。

正文第二段

adverse (adj.) 負面的	例 Without proper education on interpersonal relationship, peer pressure is likely to have <u>adverse</u> effects on teenagers. 沒有人際關係的妥善教育，同儕壓力對青少年可能有負面影響。 例 Some students are worried about the <u>adverse</u> effects of peer pressure because whether or not to fit in gives them anxiety. 有些學生擔心同儕壓力會有負面影響因為是否能融入這件事帶給他們焦慮。
demerit (n.) 劣勢	• **語塊 …demerit of…** 例 One of the <u>demerits</u> of teamwork is the possibility of debating heatedly with teammates. 團隊合作的劣勢之一是有可能和隊員激烈爭吵。 例 Parents are concerned that peer pressure might result in some <u>demerits</u> in their children's academic performance . 家長擔心同儕壓力可能會造成他們小孩學業上的劣勢。

incvitably (adv.) 難免地	例 <u>Inevitably</u>, youngsters might have trouble handling peer pressure. 難免地，年輕人可能會在應對同儕壓力上有麻煩。 例 In cooperation with peers, students <u>inevitably</u> debate heatedly with their group members. 在與同儕合作時，學生難免會和組員激烈地爭論。
allocate (v.) 分配	• **語塊 …allocate…for…** 例 Students might <u>allocate</u> money <u>for</u> luxury goods because of peer pressure. 學生可能會因同儕壓力而分配錢來購買奢侈品。 例 Youngsters are likely to become envious and start <u>allocating</u> their time and money in order to keep up with their friends. 年輕人有可能會變得嫉妒而開始分配時間和金錢來追上朋友的腳步。
squander (v) 揮霍	• **語塊 …squander 時間／金錢／機會 on…** 例 Some students might <u>squander</u> their tuition <u>on</u> buying handbags to stay fashionable and popular on campus. 有些學生可能會將他們的學費花或在買包包來校園中維持時髦與名氣。 例 Some teenagers <u>squander</u> opportunities to learn because they pay too much attention to tackling peer pressure. 有些青少年揮霍了學習的機會因為他們太專注於處理同儕壓力。
conform (vi.) 順從	• **語塊 …conform to…** 例 Teenagers <u>conform to</u> peer pressure so that they can stay in their friendship circle. 青少年順從於同儕壓力來留在他們的朋友圈內。 例 Always <u>conforming to</u> peer pressure has adverse effects on the emotional development of teenagers. 總是順從同儕壓力對青少年的情緒發展有負面的影響。

| intact (adj.)
完整無缺的 | 例 Students are pressured to conform to others to keep their friendship intact.
學生被迫要順從他人來保有他們的友誼。 |
| | 例 Due to peer pressure, some teenagers are unable to tell right from wrong. Keeping their friendship intact is the top priority.
由於同儕壓力，有些學生不能分辨是非。維持他們的友誼是最高優先。 |

結論	
harness (v.) 控制	例 Peer pressure can still be beneficial to teenagers as long as they harnessed it properly. 只要青少年能妥善控制同儕壓力，它就能對他們有益。
	例 Harnessing the force of peer pressure is the key to having a good interpersonal relationship at school. 控制同儕壓力的影響是能在學校擁有良好人際關係的關鍵。
self-actualization (n.) 自我實現	例 Through active cooperation with peers, students are able to pursue self-actualization with stronger determination. 透過與同儕的積極合作，學生能有更強的決心來追求自我實現。
	例 Youngsters should be aware of how to take advantage of peer pressure to make it a driving force for self-actualization. 年輕人應該要知道如何利用同儕壓力來讓它成為一股追求自我實現的動力。

結構性語塊

導論	■ **表達立場**：As far as Sb beV concerned, S + V. **e.g.,As far as I am concerned,** the advantages of having peer pressure outweigh the disadvantages.
正文第一段	■ **說明一個面向**：On the one hand, S + V. e.g.,**On the one hand**, peer pressure can bring massive advantages to youngsters. ■ **提出第一個例子**：Firstly, S + V. e.g., **Firstly,** peer pressure is able to help young people blend into the new community more easily. ■ **提出第二個例子**：Secondly, S + V. e.g.,**Secondly**, it can boost cooperation and solidarity among students in learning through teamwork and discussions. ■ **提出第三個例子**：Lastly, S + V. e.g., **Lastly,** by endeavoring to not merely improve themselves but also achieve their ambitions with peers, the young's determination becomes much greater. lead to a better life and career prospect. ■ **收尾**：S + V. e.g., They are **driven** to complete tasks together in spite of the **hurdles** ahead of them.

正文第二段	■ 說明另一個面向：On the other hand, S + V. e.g., **On the other hand**, peer pressure results in some adverse demerits. ■ 提出第一個例子：V-pp by…, S + V. e.g., Inevitably, **surrounded by** their peers, youngsters are likely to become envious and start allocating their time and money in order to keep up with their friends. ■ 提出第二個例子：In addition, S + V. e.g., **In addition**, students might be afraid of expressing personality traits genuinely in groups for fear that they might be excluded by their friends. ■ 收尾：S +V. e.g., They are pressured to **conform** to others to keep their friendship **intact**.
結論	■ 總結先讓步：In conclusion, S certainly + V… e.g., **In conclusion**, peer pressure **certainly** poses negative impacts on teenagers to some extent. ■ 再重申立場：However, S + V. e.g., **However**, it can still be beneficial as long as it is **harnessed** properly.

大綱

正文第一段	正文第二段

II. Peer pressure benefits youngsters tremendously.
 	
  A. It helps young people blend into new community more easily.
 	
  B. It can boost cooperation and solidarity.
 	
  C. Young people's determination can become stronger.
	III. Peer pressure can influence teenagers negatively.
	
	  A. Youngsters are likely to allocate time and money to keep up with their friends because they are jealous.
	
	  B. Students are afraid of being who they are because they want to fit in.

優劣勢（二）

You should spend about 40 minutes on this task.

More and more people prefer having children later in life. What are the reasons? Do the advantages outweigh the disadvantages?

Give reasons for your answer and include any relevant examples from your own knowledge or experience.

Write at least 250 words.

範文

It is true that much more couples tend to **delay** having children after getting married for different reasons. Even though there are **drawbacks**, they are outweighed by the benefits.

Newlyweds prefer delaying childbirth because of different factors. To begin with, having babies later offers young couples **ample** time and opportunities to enjoy their lives fully. They can step out of their **comfort zones** to engage in a variety of activities for entertainment or self-actualization. For instance, **taking up** sports or climbing the employment ladder. Clearly, they are more likely to have diverse experiences and **progress** more rapidly in their career. Employment status is another factor that **puts** childbirth **on hold**. **Competition** in the job market is much fiercer, so couples need to concentrate on their work to secure their positions in the workplace instead of taking on parental roles.

On the one hand, there are disadvantages to having children late. First of all, the risks of suffering from potential health problems or even death should not be ignored. Having babies later is reported to **pose** negative impacts on future **offspring**, such as personality disorder. On the other, there are massive advantages. Newlyweds are **exempt** from the burden of child care to manage their lives as couples as well as individuals. They have the luxury to center their lives around professional career. What is more, they are given the chance to pursue their passions. For instance, learning languages or anything they are **fascinated** by before **embarking** on parenthood.

Though young people decide to delay childbirth for different reasons, I am **convinced** that the advantages outweigh the disadvantages.

☝ 內容性語塊

導論

delay (v) 延遲	• **語塊 …delay…for…** 例 A majority of young couples <u>delay</u> having children <u>for</u> their career. 多數的年輕伴侶為了他們的職涯而延遲生育。 • **用法 …delay V-ing** 例 More couples tend to <u>delay having</u> children after getting married for different reasons. 更多的伴侶因不同因素傾向婚後晚生小孩。

drawback (n.) 缺點	● **語塊 …drawback of…** 例 One of the <u>drawbacks of</u> having children early is having limited time to pursue career goals. 早生小孩的缺點之一就是能追求職涯目標的時間有限。 例 The benefits of delaying giving birth to children outweigh the <u>drawbacks</u>. 晚生小孩的好處多於缺點。

<table>
<tr><td colspan="2">正文第一段</td></tr>
<tr>
<td>newlyweds (n.) 結婚新人</td>
<td>例 Some <u>newlyweds</u> prioritize having children over their career while others consider the otherwise.
有些結婚新人將生育排在他們的職涯之前，而其他持相反意見。

例 Most <u>newlyweds</u> delay having children because they want more quality time as husbands and wives.
多數結婚新人晚生小孩因為他們想要更多當夫妻的美好時光。</td>
</tr>
<tr>
<td>prefer (v.) 偏好</td>
<td>● 語塊 …prefer…to…

例 Some couples <u>prefer</u> career <u>to</u> children.
有些伴侶偏好工作勝過小孩。

● 用法 …prefer V-ing/to V

例 Other couples <u>prefer giving/to give</u> birth to children early.
其他伴侶偏好早生小孩。</td>
</tr>
</table>

ample (adj.) 充裕的	• 搭配詞 **ample time/evidence/opportunity** 例 Having babies later offers young couples <u>ample time and opportunities</u> to enjoy their lives fully. 晚生小孩提供年輕伴侶充裕的時間和機會來完整享受他們的生活。 例 More and more couples decide not to give birth to children early because they want <u>ample</u> time for managing their career development. 越來越多的伴侶決定不早生小孩因為他們想要充裕的時間來管理他們的職涯發展。
comfort zone (n.) 舒適圈	例 Not having children early in life offers newlyweds the chance to step out of their <u>comfort zones</u>. 晚生小孩提供結婚新人機會去踏出他們的舒適圈。 例 Through stepping out of their <u>comfort zones</u>, young couples can understand who they are better and develop essential skills for success in the workplace. 藉由踏出他們的舒適圈，年輕伴侶能更加瞭解自己及培養能在職場成功的必要技能。
take up (v.) 培養；從事	例 Delaying having children allows newlyweds the time to <u>take up</u> other interests. 晚生小孩允許結婚新人有時間培養其他的興趣。 例 Newlyweds can step out of their comfort zones to engage in a variety of activities, such as <u>taking up</u> sports. 結婚新人能踏出他們的舒適圈來進行各式各樣的活動，像是從事運動。

progress (v.) 進展	• **語塊 …progress to V-ing/N.** 例 By delaying childbirth, couples have more time to <u>progress to getting</u> themselves in better positions in the workplace. 透過晚生小孩，伴侶有更多時間來讓自己在職場進展到更好的職位。 例 Newlyweds are more likely to have diverse experiences and <u>progress</u> more rapidly in their career 結婚新人更有可能有多樣的經驗並在職涯中進展更快。
put…on hold (v.) 暫緩	例 Due to financial challenges, the couple decided to <u>put</u> childbirth <u>on hold</u>. 由於經濟上的挑戰，這對伴侶決定暫緩生育。 例 <u>Putting</u> childbirth <u>on hold</u> should be a mutual decision made by the couple 暫緩生育應是伴侶共同做出的決定。
competition (n.) 競爭	• **搭配詞 stiff/tough/fierce competition** 例 As <u>competition</u> is getting much <u>fiercer</u> in the job market, most couples decide to delay giving birth to children. 隨著職場的競爭變得更加激烈，多數的伴侶決定晚生小孩。 例 <u>Competition</u> in the job market is much <u>fiercer</u>, so couples need to concentrate on their work to secure their positions in the workplace instead of taking on parental roles. 職場中的競爭變得更加激烈，所有伴侶需要專注在工作上來保住他們的職位，而不是當父母。

正文第二段	
pose **(v.)** 造成	• **用法** …pose impacts on… 例 Having children later <u>poses negative impacts on</u> women. 晚生小孩對女性造成負面影響。 例 Experts suggest that newlyweds should not delay childbirth to avoid <u>posing negative impacts on</u> the mother and child. 專家建議結婚新人不應晚生小孩以避免對媽媽和小孩有負面影響。
offspring (n.) 後代	例 Having babies later is reported to pose negative impacts on future <u>offspring</u>, such as personality disorder. 據報導晚生小孩會對後代造成負面影響，像是人格失調。 例 Some couples try to have babies early so as to prevent their <u>offspring</u> from any types of health problems. 有些伴侶嘗試早生小孩為了避免小孩有任何的健康問題。
exempt (adj.) 免除的	• **語塊** …be exempt from… 例 If newlyweds have children later, they <u>are exempt from</u> the burden of child care to manage their lives as couples as well as individuals. 如果結婚新人晚生小孩，他們就免除了養育小孩的負擔而能管理他們作為伴侶以及個人的生活。 例 Once couples have children, they cannot <u>be exempt from</u> taking full responsibility as parents. 只要伴侶有小孩，他們就沒辦法免除作為父母的責任。

fascinated (adj.) 感興趣的	• **語塊** …be fascinated by… 例 Young couples <u>are</u> still <u>fascinated by</u> different activities, so giving birth to children might not be their top priority. 年輕伴侶仍對不同活動感興趣，因此生小孩或許不是他們的優先考量。 例 <u>Being fascinated by</u> children is one thing, raising them is quite another. 對小孩感興趣是一回事，而養育他們完全是另一回事。
embark (vi.) 展開；上船	• **語塊** …embark on… 例 Before <u>embarking on</u> parenthood, couples should consider a myriad of factors carefully. 在開始當父母前，伴侶要仔細考量許多因素。 例 Newlywed should be prepared physically, emotionally, and financially so as to <u>embark on</u> their journey as parents smoothly. 結婚新人應要在身體、心情和經濟上做好準備來展開作為父母的旅程。

結論

convinced (adj.) 確信的	• **語塊** …be convinced of… 例 Knowing the health risks of delaying childbirth, the newlyweds <u>are convinced of</u> doing it as early as possible. 了解晚生小孩的健康風險後，結婚新人確信要盡可能越早生。 例 I <u>am convinced that</u> the advantages of delaying having children outweigh the disadvantages. 我確信晚生小孩的優勢多於劣勢。

🍸 結構性語塊

導論	■ 表達立場：Even though S + V, S +V. **e.g., Even though** there are drawbacks, they are outweighed by the benefits.
正文第一段	■ 主題句：S + V because of…factors. e.g., Newlyweds prefer delaying childbirth **because of** different **factors**. ■ 提出第一個例子：To begin with, S + V. e.g., **To begin with**, having babies later offers young couples ample time and opportunities to enjoy their lives fully. ■ 提出第二個例子：S + V is another factor that... e.g., Employment status **is another factor that** puts childbirth on hold.
正文第二段	■ 說明第一個面向：On the one hand, S + V. e.g., **On the one hand**, there are disadvantages to having children late. ■ 提出第二個面向：On the other, S + V. e.g., **On the other**, there are massive advantages.
結論	■ 先讓步再總結：Though S + V, S + V. e.g., **Though** young people decide to delay childbirth for different reasons, I am convinced that the advantages outweigh the disadvantages.

大綱

正文第一段	正文第二段

II. Young couples prefer having kids later.
  A. They have more time and opportunities to do what they want.
  B. They can progress fast in the workplace.
  C. They can focus on keeping their positions.
	III. The advantages and disadvantages of having children later
	  A. It poses negative impacts on offspring.
	  B. Couples have the luxury to focus on their career.
	  C. They can pursue their passions.

問題與解決方法（一）

You should spend about 40 minutes on this task.

Traffic congestion is becoming a huge problem for many major cities. What are the causes? Suggest some measures to reduce traffic in big cities.

Give reasons for your answer and include any relevant examples from your own knowledge or experience.

Write at least 250 words.

範文

In recent years, traffic **congestion** has become an enormous **obstacle** for modern citizens. In this essay, I will discuss several reasons that contribute to the situation and suggest different **remedies** that could be used to **tackle** the problem.

The increasing congestion in metropolitan areas results from two main causes. A **surge** in population could be regarded as the first **culprit**. A considerable number of people have **migrated** to reside in urban areas, such as Beijing, Tokyo, or New York. This brings about an **excessive** number of commuters who travel in cities and **overcrowd** the streets every day. The second explanation could be that individuals prefer using private vehicles rather than public transport because of convenience and flexibility. Therefore, these reasons cause traffic congestion during **peak** hours in big cities.

Traffic congestion could be **mitigated** via different measures. Firstly, governments should draw up **budgets** for improving public transport as well as the **infrastructure**. By **upgrading** the transport system, it would encourage residents to travel by bus, train or subway rather than their own vehicles. With fewer vehicles on roads, it could eventually **alleviate** the situation of traffic congestion. In addition, **imposing** higher taxes or charging congestion fee could partly solve the issue. These regulations could discourage individuals from driving private transport into the city center.

In conclusion, there are two main contributors to traffic congestion and the above solutions should be **implemented** immediately to **address** this modern-day problem.

☞ 內容性語塊

導論	
congestion (n.) 擁塞	例 The mayor and his team are working on reducing traffic <u>congestion</u> in the city. 市長與他的團隊正在處理市內交通堵塞的問題。 例 Traffic <u>congestion</u> troubles people as it makes them anxious about not being on time for work or school. 塞車困擾人們因為這讓他們為不能準時上班或上課感到焦慮。

obstacle (n.) 障礙	• **語塊 …obstacle to…** 例 Traffic congestion is one of the <u>obstacles to</u> progress of the city. 塞車是阻擋城市進步的阻礙之一。 • **搭配詞 a major/serious obstacle** 例 Both the government and citizens should work hand in hand to overcome <u>serious obstacles</u>, such as traffic congestion. 政府和市民必須聯手來克服各種嚴重的挑戰，像是交通阻塞。
remedy (n) 補救	• **語塊 …remedy for…** 例 The city government has proposed a variety of <u>remedies for</u> traffic congestion, but all to no avail. 市政府已經為塞車提出各式的補救方法，但沒有一個有用。 例 With the <u>remedies</u> suggested by the government, citizens should also be responsible for putting them into practice. 有了政府建議的補救方法，市民應要負責執行它們。
tackle (v.) 處理	• **搭配詞 tackle a problem/issue/question** 例 We must understand the reasons that contributed to congestions before <u>tackling</u> it. 在處理塞車問題前，我們一定要瞭解導致它的原因。 • **搭配詞 tackle…head-on.** 例 Through <u>tackling</u> the causes and consequences of traffic congestion <u>head-on</u>, people in the city finally can commute much more efficiently. 藉由迎頭處理塞車的原因和後果，都市的的人們終於能更有效率地通勤。

surge (n.) 驟升	• **語塊 …a surge in…** 例 <u>A surge in</u> population could be regarded as the main reason that leads to traffic congestion. 人口的驟升可被視為導致塞車的主要原因。 例 An increasing number of people contributes to <u>a surge in</u> private vehicles simultaneously. 人口的持續增加同時導致私有車輛的驟升。
culprit (n.) 罪魁禍首	例 Most people consider the increasing population the main <u>culprit</u> for traffic congestion. 大多人視持續上升的人口為塞車的罪魁禍首。 例 Another <u>culprit</u> for traffic congestion is private vehicles because they fill all the roads of the city during rush hours. 另一個導致塞車的罪魁禍首是私有車因為它們在尖峰時段塞滿街道。
migrate (v.) 移居	例 With more and more people <u>migrating</u> to Taipei, overpopulation becomes a serious problem. 隨著越來越多人移居到台北，人口過剩變成一個嚴重的問題。 例 Traffic congestion is a trouble for many cities because people keep <u>migrating</u> from elsewhere. 塞車是許多都市的困擾因為人們持續從其他地方移居過來。
excessive (adj.) 過多的	• **搭配詞 an excessive use of sth.** 例 <u>An excessive use of</u> private vehicles is the main culprit of congestion. 過量使用私有車是塞車的罪魁禍首。 例 The underdeveloped transport system causes the <u>excessive use of</u> private vehicles. 未完全開發的運輸系統導致私有車的過量使用。

overcrowd (v.) 充斥	例 Buses, taxis, and private vehicles <u>overcrowd</u> the city during rush hours. 公車、計程車以及私有車在尖峰時段充斥著城市。 例 Once people find public transport convenient, they can stop private vehicles from <u>overcrowding</u> the city. 只要人們覺得大眾運輸方便，他們就能讓私有車輛不再充斥著城市。
peak (adj.) 尖峰的	例 These reasons cause traffic congestion during <u>peak</u> hours in big cities. 這些原因導致大城市在尖峰時段塞車。 例 If you want to arrive on time, I suggest avoiding commuting during <u>peak</u> hours. 如果你想要準時抵達，我建議不要在尖峰時段通勤。

正文第二段

mitigate (v.) 緩解	例 Traffic congestion could be <u>mitigated</u> via different measures. 塞車可透過不同措施來緩解。 例 The city government came up with measures to <u>mitigate</u> traffic congestion. 市政府提出措施來緩解塞車。
budget (n.) 預算	• 搭配詞 **draw up a budget for...** 例 The government should <u>draw up a budget for</u> public transport so that people drive their own vehicles less often. 市政府應為大眾運輸編列預算以讓人們降低開自己車的頻率。 例 To tackle the problem of traffic congestion, the government should <u>draw up a</u> reasonable <u>budget</u>. 為了處理塞車的問題，政府應編列合理的預算。

infrastructure (n.) 基礎建設	例 Traffic congestion often happens in cities with poorly developed infrastructure. 塞車經常在基礎建設開發不善的城市發生。 例 If the infrastructure can be developed better, traffic congestion might not be as troublesome as it is now. 如果基礎建設能被開發地更好，塞車或許就不會如現在這麼令人困擾。
upgrade (v.) 升級	例 By upgrading the transport system, it would encourage residents to travel by bus, train or subway rather than their own vehicles. 透過升級運輸系統，這能鼓勵居民搭公車、火車或地鐵而不開他們自己的車。 例 The key to mitigating traffic congestion is asking the city government to upgrade the transport system. 緩解塞車的關鍵是要求市政府升級運輸系統。
alleviate (v.) 減輕	例 Traffic congestion could be alleviated via different measures. 塞車可透過不同措施來緩解。 例 The city government came up with measures to alleviate traffic congestion. 市政府提出措施來緩解塞車。
impose (v.) 強加	• 搭配詞 impose a ban/tax/burden/strain on… 例 Imposing higher taxes or charging congestion fee could partly solve the issue. 強加更高的稅或收塞車費或許能解決部分的問題。 例 Imposing a ban on private vehicles is too drastic a measure. 強加私有車輛的禁令是一個過於激進的措施。

結論	
implement (v.) 執行	例 It takes both the government and citizens to implement these measures to cope with traffic congestion. 要執行能處理塞車的措施需要政府和市民的幫忙。 例 Implementing the measures in full is essential to alleviate traffic congestion. 為了緩解塞車，有必要徹底執行這些措施。
address (v.) 處理	• 搭配詞 **address a problem/question/issue** 例 The above solutions should be implemented immediately to address this modern-day problem. 以上的這些措施應要立刻執行來處理這現代的問題。 例 Addressing traffic congestion takes much more time because different factors must be put into consideration. 處理塞車花費了更多的時間因為不同的因素都要被納入考量。

🐮 結構性語塊

導論	■ 提出文章目的：In this essay, I will discuss… **e.g.,In this essay, I will discuss** several reasons that contribute to the situation and suggest different remedies that could be used to tackle the problem.

正文第一段	■ 主題句：A result from B. e.g., The increasing congestion in metropolitan areas **results from** two main causes. ■ 提出第一個例子：A could be regarded as the first... e.g., A surge in population **could be regarded as the first** culprit. ■ 提出第二個例子：The second explanation could be... e.g., **The second explanation could be** that individuals prefer using private vehicles rather than public transport because of convenience and flexibility.
正文第二段	■ 主題句：A could be mitigated via... e.g.,Traffic congestion **could be mitigated via** different measures. ■ 提出第一個例子：**Firstly, S + V.** e.g., **Firstly**, governments should draw up budgets for improving public transport as well as the infrastructure. ■ 提出第二個例子：**In addition, S + V.** e.g., **In addition**, imposing higher taxes or charging congestion fee could partly solve the issue.
結論	■ 總結：In conclusion, S + V. e.g., **In conclusion**, there are two main contributors to traffic congestion and the above solutions should be implemented immediately to address this modern-day problem.

正文第一段	正文第二段
II. Causes of traffic congestion 　　A. A surge in population 　　B. People prefer driving their own cars.	III. Solutions to traffic congestion 　　A. The government should spend money improving public transport and infrastructure. 　　B. Imposing taxes or charging congestion fee

問題與解決方法（二）

You should spend about 40 minutes on this task.

In recent years, there has been a considerable rise in crimes committed by young people in cities. What has caused this? What solutions can you suggest?

Give reasons for your answer and include any relevant examples from your own knowledge or experience.

Write at least 250 words.

✏️ 範文

Recently, the rise of crime among **adolescents** is an urgent problem in cities. This essay will discuss reasons behind this issue and propose some **feasible** solutions.

The rise in crimes **committed** by young people result from two primary causes. The first reason is that drugs and alcohol are generally sold at low prices that enable youngsters to buy them and use them. It is undeniable that people could easily lose control because of abuse of drugs and alcohol. For instance, street fights often take place outside bars and clubs. Another reason is that teenagers nowadays are under **immense** pressure from their parents who demand them to **excel** at their academic performance. Such pressure could make them **go astray** and hang out with **delinquents** to escape from reality. Without their own **moral compass**, they might end up committing serious crimes easily.

Measures must be implemented to tackle this problem. Firstly, a stricter system of **penalties** should be established to **deter** adolescents from crimes. It is reported that countries with **tighter** laws have lower crimes rates than the others. Secondly, schools must teach teenagers moral values, such as tolerance and sharing. For example, time on studying math or English could be reduced and filled in with other practical classes. This could raise **awareness** of telling right from wrong among students, and eventually it could lower crime rates.

In conclusion, various measures can be **taken into account** to tackle the surge in teenage crimes.

☝ 內容性語塊

導論	
adolescent (n.) 青少年	例 Recently, the rise of crime among <u>adolescents</u> is an urgent problem in cities. 青少年犯罪的增加是近期都市中急迫的問題。 例 Teachers and parents should pay much more attention to the mental health of <u>adolescents</u> so that they do not make decisions that they will regret later. 老師和家長應要更加注意青少年的心理健康好讓他們不會做出以後會後悔的決定。
feasible (adj.) 可行的	例 The government and schools should come up with <u>feasible</u> solutions to the rise of crimes among teenagers. 政府和學校應想出應對青少年犯罪上升的可行辦法。 例 When proposing solutions, we must consider how <u>feasible</u> they are so as to implement them fully. 當提出解決方法時，我們一定要考量是否可行才能全面地執行。

commit (v) 犯下	• 搭配詞 **commit a crime/an offense** 例 Without sufficient education and care, adolescents are more likely to commit crimes. 沒有足夠的教育和關心，青少年更有可能犯罪。 例 The rise in crimes committed by young people results from two primary causes. 青少年犯罪的上升可能出自於兩個主要的原因。
immense (adj.) 巨大的	例 Immense pressure from parents is one of the primary reasons that leads to crimes among teenagers. 來自父母巨大的壓力是導致青少年犯罪的主要原因之一。 例 Teenagers might regard committing crimes as an outlet for the immense pressure from schools. 青少年可能視犯罪為發洩來自學校巨大壓力的出口。
excel (vi.) 擅長；表現出色	• 語塊 **…excel at…** 例 Most adolescents are required to excel at their academic performance. 多數的青少年被要求在學業表現要出色。 例 Some adolescents cannot cope with the pressure of having to excel at school and end up committing suicide or crimes. 有些青少年無法應付被要求在學校得表現出色的壓力而落得犯罪或自殺的下場。
go astray (v.) 誤入歧途	例 Immense pressure from parents could lead teenagers to go astray. 來自父母的巨大壓力可能導致青少年誤入歧途。 例 Teenagers who go astray often suffer from substance abuse. 誤入歧途的青少年經常有遭受藥物濫用之苦。

delinquent (n.) 少年犯	例 Parents and teachers should be partially responsible for the misconduct of delinquents. 家長和老師應對少年犯的過失負起部分的責任。 例 Delinquents may encourage adolescents who experience immense pressure to go astray with them. 少年犯可能會慫恿壓力的青少年與他們一起誤入歧途。
moral compass (n.) 道德指標	例 Without their own moral compass, youngsters are misguided easily by delinquents. 沒有他們自己的道德指標，青少年很容易被少年犯誤導。 例 Youngsters should receive proper education on moral and ethics to develop their own moral compass. 青少年應接受有關道德與倫理的教育來發展他們自己的道德指標。

正文第二段

penalty (v.) 刑罰	• 搭配詞 **a severe/tough/harsh penalty** 例 Tougher penalties should be established to stop adolescents from crimes. 更嚴厲的刑罰應被設立來阻止青少年犯罪。 • 搭配詞 **impose a penalty** 例 Imposing tougher penalties can remind teenagers that there will be consequences for any types of misconducts. 施行更嚴厲的刑罰能提醒青少年任何種類的過失都會有後果。
deter (v.) 使不敢	• 語塊 **…deter someone from V-ing** 例 Harsher penalties should be established to deter adolescents from committing crimes. 更嚴厲的刑罰該被設立來讓青少年不敢犯罪。 例 Deterring adolescents from crimes requires joint efforts from teachers and parents. 嚇阻青少年犯罪需要老師和家長共同的努力。

tight (adj.) 嚴格的	例 It is reported that countries with <u>tighter</u> laws have lower crimes rates than the others. 據報導有更嚴厲法律的國家比他國的犯罪率都低。 例 Imposing <u>tighter</u> laws deters youngsters from committing crimes. 執行更加嚴厲的法律能使青少年不敢犯罪。
awareness (n.) 意識	• 搭配詞 **raise awareness of** 例 Educating adolescents on moral and ethics <u>raises</u> their <u>awareness of</u> telling right from wrong. 教青少年倫理與道德能提升對分辨是非的意識。 例 <u>Raising awareness of</u> moral and ethics should integral of education at school. 提升道德與倫理的意識應是學校教育不可或缺的一部份。

結論

take…into account (v.) 納入考量	例 Various measures can <u>be taken into account</u> to tackle the surge in teenage crimes. 不同的方針應該納入考量來處理青少年犯罪的增加。 例 When guiding delinquents back to the right path, their emotions must <u>be taken into account</u>. 當引導少年犯回正軌時，他們的心情一定要被納入考量。

🐂 結構性語塊

導論	■ 提出文章目的：This essay will discuss e.g.,**This essay** will discuss reasons behind this issue and propose some feasible solutions.
正文第一段	■ 主題句：A result from B. e.g.,The rise in crimes committed by young people **result from** two primary causes. ■ 提出第一個例子：The first reason is that… e.g., **The first reason is that** drugs and alcohol are generally sold at low prices that enable youngsters to buy them and use them. ■ 提出第二個例子：Another reason is that… e.g., **Another reason is that** teenagers nowadays are under immense pressure from their parents who demand them to excel at their academic performance.
正文第二段	■ 主題句：Measures must be implemented to… e.g., **Measures must be implemented to** tackle this problem. ■ 提出第一個例子：Firstly, S + V. e.g., **Firstly**, a stricter system of penalties should be established to deter adolescents from crimes. ■ 提出第二個例子：**Secondly, S + V.** e.g., **Secondly**, schools must teach teenagers moral values, such as tolerance and sharing.
結論	■ 總結：In conclusion, S + V. e.g., **In conclusion**, various measures can be taken into account to tackle the surge in teenage crimes.

大綱

正文第一段	正文第二段
II. Causes of the rise of crimes among teenagers A. Drugs and alcohol are sold at low prices B. Teenagers are under a lot of pressure	III. Solutions to crimes among teenagers A. Imposing stricter penalties B. Schools should offer lesson on moral values

- 折線圖
- 長條圖
- 圓餅圖

I

圖表寫作練習題

折線圖

（一）、看圖填入正確的內容

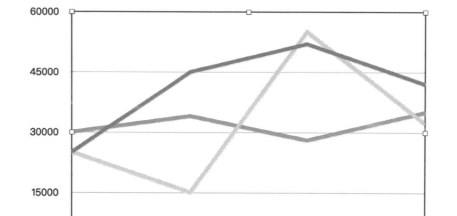

The Numbers of Stray Dogs

— Taipei　　— Taichung　　— Kaohsiung

Given is the line graph that demonstrates the number of stray dogs in Taipei, Taichung, and Kaohsiung from 2016 to 2019. Overall, Taipei had the most stray dogs and Taichung the fewest.

Increasing from about 28000, the number of stray dogs in Taipei soared _____45000 in 2017. This growth continued and reached a _____ of approximately 50000. The year 2018 _____ a gradual decr ease, _____ to 43000. The number of stray dogs in Kaohsiung remained relatively _____ in four years. It increased slightly to 32000 in 2017 and reached a _____ of 28000 in 2018. In the following year, it increased gradually to about 34000. As to the number of dogs in Taichung, the year 2017 experienced the most _____ increase, rising _____ 15000 to approximately 58000. In the _____ year, it decreased significantly _____ 27000.

（二）、詞彙資源練習

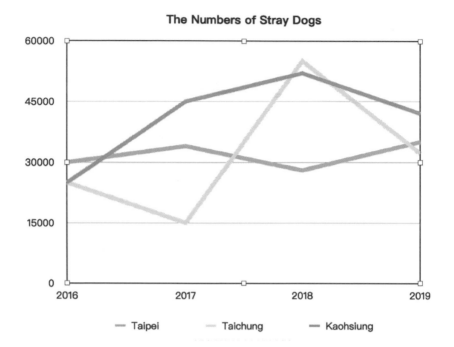

The Numbers of Stray Dogs

用指定的方式描述「台中 2017 到 2018 流浪狗」的變化

1. 用動詞

✎ _____

2. 用動詞加上副詞

✎ _____

3. 用時間當主詞

✎ _____

用指定的方式描述「高雄 2017 到 2019 流浪狗」的變化

1. 用動詞

✎ _____

2. 用動詞加上副詞

✎ _____

3. 用動詞加上語塊 …between…and…

✎ _____

長條圖

（一）、看圖填入正確的內容

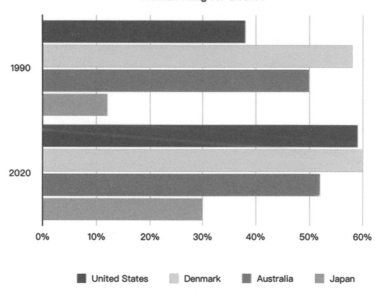

Women filing for divorce

United States   Denmark   Australia   Japan

The chart provided illustrates the percentages of women filing for divorce in four countries in 1990 and 2020. As a whole, the percentages of _____ women were the highest and Japanese the lowest in both years.

The percentage of women filing for divorce in Denmark in 2020 was almost identical to _____ in 1990, at 60% and 58% _____. The percentage of Australian women filing for divorce was quite high, _____ about 52%.

_____ , it was at 50% three decades ago. On the contrary, the percentages of American women were quite different in 2020 and 1990, with the _____ exceeding the _____ by approximately 20%. As to Japan, the percentages were at the bottom in both years. The percentage in 2020 _____ that in 1990 by 18%.

（二）、詞彙資源練習

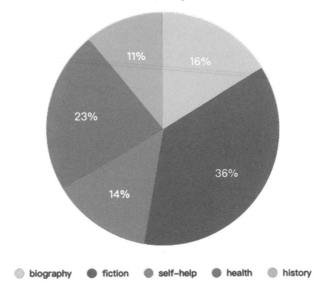

Types of books read by the students in a
university

biography ● fiction ● self-help ● health ● history

用指定方式描述「日本」兩年的婦女申請離婚率

1. 用形容詞

✎ _____

2. 用副詞

✎ _____

用指定方式比較「澳洲和美國」1990 年的婦女申請離婚率

1. 用動詞

✎ _____

2. 用形容詞

✎ _____

圓餅圖

（一）、看圖填入正確的內容

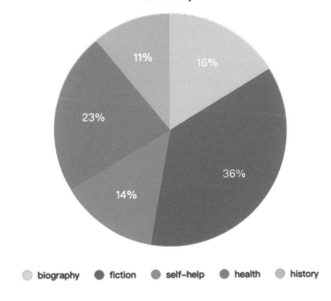

Types of books read by the students in a university

biography fiction self-help health history

Given is the pie chart that displays the types of books read by the students in a university. It is _____ of five categories, biography, fiction, self-help, health, and history. On the whole, fiction is the most popular while history is the least.

A _____ of students read fiction and health. Fiction accounts _____ a high percentage, at 36%. History _____ another high percentage, at 23%. Biography came in third and comprises 16%, which is almost twice _____ than fiction. A _____ of students read self-help and history, with the former at 14% and the latter at 11%. When these categories are compared with the majority, fiction is _____ as much as history and health is almost twice more than self-help.

（二）、詞彙資源練習

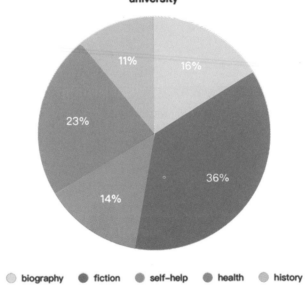

Types of books read by the students in a university

- biography
- fiction
- self-help
- health
- history

用指定方式描述「self-hep」的比例

1. 用動詞

_____

2. 用動詞和形容詞

_____

用指定方式比較「小說和傳記」的比例

1. 用同等比較

_____

2. 用比較級和副詞

_____

☝ 折線圖

（一）

Given is the line graph that demonstrates the number of stray dogs in Taipei, Taichung, and Kaohsiung from 2016 to 2019. Overall, Taipei had the most stray dogs and Taichung the fewest.

Increasing from about 28000, the number of stray dogs in Taipei soared **to** 45000 in 2017. This growth continued and reached a **summit** of approximately 50000. The year 2018 **witnessed/experienced** a gradual decrease, **falling/decreasing** to 43000. The number of stray dogs in Kaohsiung remained relatively **steady** in four years. It increased slightly to 32000 in 2017 and reached a **floor** of 28000 in 2018. In the following year, it increased gradually to about 34000. As to the number of dogs in Taichung, the year 2017 experienced the most **dramatic/considerable/ significant/substantial** increase, rising **from** 15000 to approximately 58000. In the **subsequent/following** year, it decreased significantly **by** 27000.

（二）

1. The number of stray dogs in Taichung rocketed from 15000 to about 56000.

2. The number of stray dogs in Taichung increased considerably/ dramatically/significantly/substantially to about 56000.

3. The year 2017 witness the most considerable/dramatic/significant/ substantial increase in the number of stray dogs in Taichung, rising/increasing from 15000 to about 56000.

1. Decreasing from about 32000, the number of stray dogs in Kaohsiung reached a floor of 28000 and increased to 34000.

2. The number of stray dogs in Kaohsiung decreased gradually to 28000 and increased steadily to 34000

3. The number of stray dogs in Kaohsiung fluctuated between 34000 and 28000.

長條圖

（一）

The chart provided illustrates the percentages of women filing for divorce in four countries in 1990 and 2020. As a whole, the percentages of **Danish** women were the highest and Japanesethe lowest in both years.

The percentage of women filing for divorce in Denmark in 2020 was almost identical to **that** in 1990, at 60% and 58% **respectively**. The percentage of Australian filing for divorce was quite high, **at** about 52%. **In the same way/ Similarly/Likewise**, it was at 50% three decades ago. On the contrary, the percentages of American women were quite different in 2020 and 1990, with **the former** exceeding the **latter** by approximately 20%. As to Japan, the percentages were at the bottom in both years. The percentage in 2020 **outnumbered/exceeded** that in 1990 by 18%.

（二）

1. The percentage of Japanese women filing for divorce in 2020 was superior to that in 1990 by 18%.

2. The percentage of Japanese women filing for divorce in 2020 was at 30%. Conversely, it was at 12% in 1990.

•••

1. The percentage of Australian women filing for divorce in 1990 outnumbered that of the United States by 12%.

2. The percentage of American women filing for divorce in 1990 was inferior to that of Australia by 12%.

圓餅圖

（一）

　　Given is the pie chart that displays the types of books read by the students in a university. It is **comprised** of five categories, biography, fiction, self-help, health, and history. On the whole, fiction is the most popular while history is the least.

　　A **majority** of students read fiction and health. Fiction accounts **for** a high percentage, at 36%. History **constitutes/comprises** another high percentage, at 23%. Biography came in third and comprises 16%, which is almost twice **less** than fiction. A **minority** of students read self-help and history, with the former at 14% and the latter at 11%. When these categories are compared with the majority, fiction is **three times** as much as history and health is almost twice more than self-help.

（二）

1. Self-help accounts for/comprises/constitutes 14%.
2. Self-help accounts for/comprises/constitutes a low percentage, at 14%.

1. Biography is almost three times as much as fiction, with the former at 36% and the latter at 16%.

2. Biography is three times more than fiction, at 36% and 16% respectively.

II

議論寫作練習題

同意不同意（一）

（一）、看範文填入正確的內容

It is said that students should partake _____ unpaid community services as a mandatory part of their curriculum in high schools. I strongly agree _____ this opinion based on several reasons.

To _____ with, teenagers can grow tremendously through serving the community freely. When working _____ , students learn how to solve unexpected problems without the instructions from their teachers and parents. They have the _____ to be more independent. In the meantime, teenagers involved _____ community services are able to understand that the contributions they make _____ impacts _____ others' lives. Therefore, they become much more motivated to help and more responsible _____ all the works they are assigned.

Secondly, partaking in unpaid community services provides a _____ of benefits. If students serve the community freely, especially working for a _____ foundation, they will have the opportunity to meet people from different socioeconomic backgrounds, many of whom are orphans, disabled children, or the elderly in nursing homes. Meeting these people _____ their sense of empathy for other's destiny. What is more, students come to understand the value of labor much better by performing the work without payment. They have deeper gratitude _____ what they have. If unpaid community services are made compulsory at schools, they will know how difficult it is to complete the work and stop _____ things for granted.

In conclusion, I strongly agree that participating in unpaid community services can be beneficial _____ students because it transforms them into mature, responsible, and grateful individuals.

（二）、造句練習

1. …partake in…

   ✎ _____

2. …agree with…on…

   ✎ _____

3. …be involved in…

   ✎ _____

4. …make contributions to…

   ✎ _____

5. …have an impact on…

   ✎ _____

6. …be responsible for…

   ✎ _____

7. …a myriad of…

   ✎ _____

8. …develop a sense of…

   ✎ _____

9. …have gratitude towards…

   ✎ _____

10. …be beneficial to…

   ✎ _____

同意不同意（二）

（一）、看範文填入正確的內容

It is true that salary plays an _____ part in choosing a job. However, I disagree with making it a top _____ because there are other factors that should be put into consideration.

Most people consider salary the most crucial factor when choosing a job for different reasons. Some believe that income is _____ to the quality of life. The higher you earn, the better you live. They can afford their increasing demand on not only basic needs but also luxuries, such as fashion or holidays. Other people regard salary _____ a measure of their success in the workplace. The higher income they receive, the more valuable they are. Thus, salary is front and _____ for many because it might lead to a better life and career prospect.

On the other hand, more and more people are paying _____ to other factors. First, many job seekers emphasize a healthy _____ balance. Even if their positions offer competitive salary, they still cannot stand working long hours in front of the computer every day, leaving no room for freedom and other leisure activities. In the meantime, people start choosing jobs that contribute to the society. For instance, some go to rural areas to assist and improve the performance of local enterprises _____ working for well-established companies. Although they are not paid as much, they are satisfied with their choices because they help increase the average income of the local residents. Clearly, these factors bring people a much stronger sense of satisfaction than salary.

In conclusion, it is true that salary matters. Yet, it is by no means the key consideration people should _____ to when making a career decision.

（二）、造句練習

1. …play an integral role in…

✎ _____

2. …disagree that…

✎ _____

3. …take priority over…

✎ _____

4. …put…into consideration…

✎ _____

5. …be crucial to…

✎ _____

6. …be proportional to…

✎ _____

7. …regard…as…

✎ _____

8. …pay attention to…

✎ _____

9. …assist…with…

✎ _____

10. …attend to…

✎ _____

優劣勢（一）

（一）、讀範文填入正確的內容

It is undeniable that the effects of peer pressure on youngsters have been debated _____ As far as I am concerned, the advantages of having peer pressure _____ the disadvantages.

On the one hand, peer pressure can bring massive advantages to youngsters. _____ , peer pressure is able to help young people blend into the new community more easily. Through meeting others with similar _____ and hobbies, youngsters gain a sense of belonging. Secondly, it can _____ cooperation and solidarity among students in learning through teamwork and discussions. Lastly, by endeavoring to not merely improve themselves but also achieve their ambitions with peers, the young's determination becomes much greater. They are _____ to complete tasks together in spite of the hurdles ahead of them.

On the other hand, peer pressure results in some _____ demerits. Inevitably, surrounded by their peers, youngsters are likely to become envious and start _____ their time and money in order to keep up with their friends. For instance, some students might squander their tuition on buying handbags to stay fashionable and popular on campus. In addition, students might be afraid of expressing personality traits genuinely in groups for fear that they might be excluded by their friends. They are pressured to conform _____ others to keep their friendship intact.

In conclusion, peer pressure certainly poses negative impacts on teenagers to some extent. However, it can still be beneficial as long as it is harnessed properly. Therefore, youngsters should be aware of how to take _____ of peer pressure to make it a driving force for self-actualization.

（二）、造句練習

1. …debate whether/how/what…

✎ _____

2. …a big/great/massive advantage…

✎ _____

3. …outweigh…

✎ _____

4. …put/place…at a disadvantage

✎ _____

5. …blend into…

✎ _____

6. …boost sb's confidence…

✎ _____

7. …endeavor to…

✎ _____

8. …demerit of…

✎ _____

9. …allocate…for…

✎ _____

10. …conform to…

✎ _____

優劣勢（二）

（一）、讀範文填入正確的內容

It is true that much more couples tend to delay _____ children after getting married for different reasons. Even though there are _____ , they are outweighed by the benefits.

Newlyweds _____ delaying childbirth because of different factors. To begin with, having babies later offers young couples _____ time and opportunities to enjoy their lives fully. They can step out of their comfort _____ to engage in a variety of activities for entertainment or self-actualization. For instance, taking up sports or climbing the employment ladder. Clearly, they are more likely to have diverse experiences and progress more rapidly in their career. Employment status is another factor that puts childbirth _____ hold. Competition in the job market is much fiercer, so couples need to concentrate on their work to secure their positions in the workplace instead of taking on parental roles.

On the one hand, there are disadvantages to having children late. First of all, the risks of suffering from potential health problems or even death should not be ignored. Having babies later is reported to _____ negative impacts _____ future offspring, such as personality disorder. On the other, there are massive advantages. Newlyweds are exempt _____ the burden of child care to manage their lives as couples as well as individuals. They have the luxury to center their lives around professional career. What is more, they are given the chance to pursue their passions. For instance, learning languages or anything they are fascinated by before _____ on parenthood.

Though young people decide to delay childbirth for different reasons, I am _____that the advantages outweigh the disadvantages.

（二）、造句練習

1. …delay…for…

✎ _____

2. …drawback of…

✎ _____

3. …prefer…to…

✎ _____

4. …ample time/opportunity…

✎ _____

5. …progress to…

✎ _____

6. …stiff/fierce competition

✎ _____

7. …pose impacts on…

✎ _____

8. …be exempt from…

✎ _____

9. …be fascinated by…

✎ _____

10. …embark on…

✎ _____

（一）、讀範文填入正確的內容

In recent years, traffic _____ has become an enormous obstacle for modern citizens. In this essay, I will discuss several reasons that contribute to the situation and suggest different remedies that could be used to _____ the problem.

The increasing congestion in metropolitan areas results _____ two main causes. A _____ in population could be regarded _____ the first culprit. A considerable number of people have migrated to reside in urban areas, such as Beijing, Tokyo, or New York. This brings about an _____ number of commuters who travel in cities and overcrowd the streets every day. The _____ explanation could be that individuals prefer _____ private vehicles rather than public transport because of convenience and flexibility. Therefore, these reasons cause traffic congestion during _____ hours in big cities.

Traffic congestion could be _____ via different measures. Firstly, governments should _____ up budgets for improving public transport as well as the infrastructure. By upgrading the transport system, it would encourage residents to travel by bus, train or subway rather than their own vehicles. With fewer vehicles on roads, it could eventually alleviate the situation of traffic congestion. In addition, _____ higher taxes or charging congestion fee could partly solve the issue. These regulations could discourage individuals from driving private transport into the city center.

In conclusion, there are two main contributors to traffic congestion and the above solutions should be _____ immediately to address this modern-day problem.

（二）、造句練習

1. …obstacle to…

✎ _____

2. …remedy for…

✎ _____

3. …tackle a problem/issue/question

✎ _____

4. …a surge in…

✎ _____

5. …an excessive use of…

✎ _____

6. …draw up a budget for…

✎ _____

7. …impose a ban/tax/burden/strain on…

✎ _____

8. …alleviate…

✎ _____

9. …implement…

✎ _____

10. …address a problem/question/issue

✎ _____

問題與解決方法（二）

（一）、讀範文填入正確的內容

Recently, the rise of crime among adolescents is an urgent problem in cities. This essay will discuss reasons behind this issue and propose some _____ solutions.

The rise in crimes _____ by young people result from two primary causes. The first reason is that drugs and alcohol are generally sold at low prices that enable youngsters to buy them and use them. It is _____ that people could easily lose control because of abuse of drugs and alcohol. For instance, street fights often take place outside bars and clubs. _____ reason is that teenagers nowadays are under _____ pressure from their parents who demand them to excel _____ their academic performance. Such pressure could make them go astray and hand out with delinquents to escape from reality. Without their own moral _____ , they might end up committing serious crimes easily.

Measures must be implemented to tackle this problem. Firstly, a stricter system of penalties should be established to deter adolescents _____ .crimes. It is reported that countries with _____ laws have lower crimes rates than the others. Secondly, schools must teach teenagers moral values, such as tolerance and sharing. For example, time on studying math or English could be reduced and filled in with other practical classes. This could _____ awareness of telling right from wrong among students, and eventually it could lower crime rates.

In conclusion, various measures can be taken into _____ to tackle the surge in teenage crimes.

（二）、造句練習

1. …adolescent…

✎ _____

2. …feasible…

✎ _____

3. …commit a crime/an offense…

✎ _____

4. …immense…

✎ _____

5. …excel at…

✎ _____

6. …go astray…

✎ _____

7. …delinquent…

✎ _____

8. …a severe/tough/harsh penalty…

✎ _____

9. …deter…from…

✎ _____

10. …raise awareness of…

✎ _____

11. …take into account…

✎ _____

✓ 參考答案

☞ 同意不同意（一）

It is said that students should partake **in** unpaid community services as a mandatory part of their curriculum in high schools. I strongly agree **with** this opinion based on several reasons.

To **begin** with, teenagers can grow tremendously through serving the community freely. When working **voluntarily**, students learn how to solve unexpected problems without the instructions from their teachers and parents. They have the **opportunity** to be more independent. In the meantime, teenagers involved **in** community services are able to understand that the contributions they make **have** impacts **on** others' lives. Therefore, they become much more motivated to help and more responsible **for** all the works they are assigned.

Secondly, partaking in unpaid community services provides a **myriad** of benefits. If students serve the community freely, especially working for a **charitable** foundation, they will have the opportunity to meet people from different socioeconomic backgrounds, many of whom are orphans, disabled children, or the elderly in nursing homes. Meeting these people **develops** their sense of empathy for other's destiny. What is more, students come to understand the value of labor much better by performing the work without payment. They have deeper gratitude **towards** what they have. If unpaid community services are made compulsory at schools, they will know how difficult it is to complete the work and stop **taking** things for granted.

In conclusion, I strongly agree that participating in unpaid community services can be beneficial **to** students because it transforms them into mature, responsible, and grateful individuals.

同意不同意（二）

It is true that salary plays an **integral** part in choosing a job. However, I disagree with making it a top **priority** because there are other factors that should be put into consideration.

Most people consider salary the most crucial factor when choosing a job for different reasons. Some believe that income is **proportional** to the quality of life. The higher you earn, the better you live. They can afford their increasing demand on not only basic needs but also luxuries, such as fashion or holidays. Other people regard salary **as** a measure of their success in the workplace. The higher income they receive, the more valuable they are. Thus, salary is front and **center** for many because it might lead to a better life and career prospect.

On the other hand, more and more people are paying **attention** to other factors. First, many job seekers emphasize a healthy **work-life** balance. Even if their positions offer competitive salary, they still cannot stand working long hours in front of the computer every day, leaving no room for freedom and other leisure activities. In the meantime, people start choosing jobs that contribute to the society. For instance, some go to rural areas to assist and improve the performance of local enterprises **instead of** working for well-established companies. Although they are not paid as much, they are satisfied with their choices because they help increase the average income of the local residents. Clearly, these factors bring people a much stronger sense of satisfaction than salary.

In conclusion, it is true that salary matters. Yet, it is by no means the key consideration people should **attend** to when making a career decision.

👆 優劣勢（一）

It is undeniable that the effects of peer pressure on youngsters have been debated **heatedly**. As far as I am concerned, the advantages of having peer pressure **outweigh** the disadvantages.

On the one hand, peer pressure can bring massive advantages to youngsters. **Firstly**, peer pressure is able to help young people blend into the new community more easily. Through meeting others with similar **characteristics** and hobbies, youngsters gain a sense of belonging. Secondly, it can **boost** cooperation and solidarity among students in learning through teamwork and discussions. Lastly, by endeavoring to not merely improve themselves but also achieve their ambitions with peers, the young's determination becomes much greater. They are **driven** to complete tasks together in spite of the hurdles ahead of them.

On the other hand, peer pressure results in some **adverse** demerits. Inevitably, surrounded by their peers, youngsters are likely to become envious and start **allocating** their time and money in order to keep up with their friends. For instance, some students might squander their tuition on buying handbags to stay fashionable and popular on campus. In addition, students might be afraid of expressing personality traits genuinely in groups for fear that they might be excluded by their friends. They are pressured to conform **to** others to keep their friendship intact.

In conclusion, peer pressure certainly poses negative impacts on teenagers to some extent. However, it can still be beneficial as long as it is harnessed properly. Therefore, youngsters should be aware of how to take **advantage** of peer pressure to make it a driving force for self-actualization.

優劣勢（二）

It is true that much more couples tend to delay **having** children after getting married for different reasons. Even though there are **drawbacks**, they are outweighed by the benefits.

Newlyweds **prefer** delaying childbirth because of different factors. To begin with, having babies later offers young couples **ample** time and opportunities to enjoy their lives fully. They can step out of their comfort **zones** to engage in a variety of activities for entertainment or self-actualization. For instance, taking up sports or climbing the employment ladder. Clearly, they are more likely to have diverse experiences and progress more rapidly in their career. Employment status is another factor that puts childbirth **on** hold. Competition in the job market is much fiercer, so couples need to concentrate on their work to secure their positions in the workplace instead of taking on parental roles.

On the one hand, there are disadvantages to having children late. First of all, the risks of suffering from potential health problems or even death should not be ignored. Having babies later is reported to **pose** negative impacts **on** future offspring, such as personality disorder. On the other, there are massive advantages. Newlyweds areexempt **from** the burden of child care to manage their lives as couples as well as individuals. They have the luxury to center their lives around professional career. What is more, they are given the chance to pursue their passions. For instance, learning languages or anything they are fascinated by before **embarking** on parenthood.

Though young people decide to delay childbirth for different reasons, I am **convinced** that the advantages outweigh the disadvantages.

☝ 問題與解決方法（一）

In recent years, traffic **congestion** has become an enormous obstacle for modern citizens. In this essay, I will discuss several reasons that contribute to the situation and suggest different remedies that could be used to **tackle** the problem.

The increasing congestion in metropolitan areas results **from** two main causes. A **surge** in population could be regarded **as** the first culprit. A considerable number of people have migrated to reside in urban areas, such as Beijing, Tokyo, or New York. This brings about an **excessive** number of commuters who travel in cities and overcrowd the streets every day. The **second** explanation could be that individuals prefer **using** private vehicles rather than public transport because of convenience and flexibility. Therefore, these reasons cause traffic congestion during **peak** hours in big cities.

Traffic congestion could be **mitigated** via different measures. Firstly, governments should **draw** up budgets for improving public transport as well as the infrastructure. By upgrading the transport system, it would encourage residents to travel by bus, train or subway rather than their own vehicles. With fewer vehicles on roads, it could eventually alleviate the situation of traffic congestion. In addition, **imposing** higher taxes or charging congestion fee could partly solve the issue. These regulations could discourage individuals from driving private transport into the city center.

In conclusion, there are two main contributors to traffic congestion and the above solutions should be **implemented** immediately to address this modern-day problem.

🐂 問題與解決方法（二）

Recently, the rise of crime among adolescents is an urgent problem in cities. This essay will discuss reasons behind this issue and propose some **feasible** solutions.

The rise in crimes **committed** by young people result from two primary causes. The first reason is that drugs and alcohol are generally sold at low prices that enable youngsters to buy them and use them. It is **undeniable** that people could easily lose control because of abuse of drugs and alcohol. For instance, street fights often take place outside bars and clubs. **Another** reason is that teenagers nowadays are under **immense** pressure from their parents who demand them to excel **at** their academic performance. Such pressure could make them go astray and hand out with delinquents to escape from reality. Without their own moral **compass**, they might end up committing serious crimes easily.

Measures must be **implemented** to tackle this problem. Firstly, a stricter system of penalties should be established to deter adolescents **from** crimes. It is reported that countries with **tighter** laws have lower crimes rates than the others. Secondly, schools must teach teenagers moral values, such as tolerance and sharing. For example, time on studying math or English could be reduced and filled in with other practical classes. This could **raise** awareness of telling right from wrong among students, and eventually it could lower crime rates.

In conclusion, various measures can be taken into **account** to tackle the surge in teenage crimes.

語研力 *E075*

Expand：雅思學術寫作關鍵字筆記

作　　者	林政憲◎著
顧　　問	曾文旭
出版總監	陳逸祺、耿文國
主　　編	陳蕙芳
執行編輯	翁芯俐
美術編輯	李依靜
法律顧問	北辰著作權事務所

印　　製	世和印製企業有限公司
初　　版	2022 年 12 月
出　　版	凱信企業集團 - 凱信企業管理顧問有限公司
電　　話	（02）2773-6566
傳　　真	（02）2778-1033
地　　址	106 台北市大安區忠孝東路四段 218 之 4 號 12 樓
信　　箱	kaihsinbooks@gmail.com

定　　價	新台幣 360 元 / 港幣 120 元
產品內容	1 書

總 經 銷	采舍國際有限公司
地　　址	235 新北市中和區中山路二段 366 巷 10 號 3 樓
電　　話	（02）8245-8786
傳　　真	（02）8245-8718

國家圖書館出版品預行編目資料

Expand：雅思學術寫作關鍵字筆記/林政憲著. – 初
版. – 臺北市：凱信企業集團凱信企業管理顧問有限
公司, 2022.12
　　面；　公分
ISBN 978-626-7097-50-2(平裝)
1.CST: 國際英語語文測試系統 2.CST: 作文

805.189　　　　　　　　　　　　　　111017928